Gunnison drove up his knee with the one-armed man's groin as his target. He missed, but his knee hit him at the base of his slightly overhanging belly. The fleshy mass absorbed the blow like a pillow.

Still, it hurt him enough to make him fall back. Gunnison dug beneath his vest for the small knife sheathed there. The three-inch blade glittered in the light from the street. Gunnison chuckled to see a flash of fear in his face. This one-armed devil would run from him now.

He didn't. Instead he glared at Gunnison, breathing louder and faster like he was trying to inflate himself. "Think to scare me off with that, do you?" he growled. Then another blade glittered, this one eight inches long and in his hand, not Gunnison's. It was his turn to chuckle. Gunnison's knife suddenly felt like a toy.

"Boy, you'd best find a bucket to tote your bowels in!" The knife sliced toward Gunnison's abdomen. The man laughed again. . . .

# THE HANGING AT LEADVILLE

## Cameron Judd

BANTAM BOOKS
NEW YORK · TORONTO · LONDON · SYDNEY · AUCKLAND

THE HANGING AT LEADVILLE
*A Bantam Domain Book / October 1991*

*DOMAIN and the portrayal of a boxed "d" are trademarks
of Bantam Books, a division of Bantam Doubleday Dell
Publishing Group, Inc.*

ISBN 0-553-28846-6

*Published simultaneously in the United States and Canada*

*Bantam Books are published by Bantam Books, a division of
Bantam Doubleday Dell Publishing Group, Inc. Its trademark,
consisting of the words "Bantam Books" and the portrayal of a
rooster, is Registered in U.S. Patent and Trademark Office and
in other countries. Marca Registrada. Bantam Books, 666 Fifth
Avenue, New York, New York 10103.*

PRINTED IN THE UNITED STATES OF AMERICA

RAD    0 9 8 7 6 5 4 3 2 1

*For Richard Curtis: agent, educator, and encourager*

# THE
# HANGING
# AT
# LEADVILLE

# Prologue

The music started just after sunset, rising up from a single voice that was as high as the surrounding Colorado peaks and as pure as the air had been before the smelters were built. A throng of men, women, and children stood and sat in the clearing before the makeshift stage and let themselves fall under the musical spell of the guitar-strumming singer. He was a rotund man with a shock of thick, strawy hair and the appropriately melodic name of Mickey Scarborough.

Entertainment was abundant in the town of Leadville, but most of it was not of the quality of the Western Warblemaster, as Scarborough coyly billed himself. Two weeks ago, the first notice of Scarborough's impending performance had been published in the Leadville newspapers, and from Malta to Stray Horse Gulch, the people of the mountains had marked their calendars not to miss his show. Mickey Scarborough was reputed to be a fine performer, with a peculiar quavering tenor voice and a charisma to rival that of his more famous peer, Eddie Foy.

Even so, it was not solely the quality of his show that accounted for his appeal. Almost equally attractive was a certain well-publicized element of mystery sur-

1

rounding Scarborough's unusual voice. His throat, the story had it, had been injured at some time or another, giving him a voice with an eerie, effortless vibrato and a remarkably high range. The mystery involved the nature of the injury, and Scarborough, with his showman's instinct, played the enigma as skillfully as he did his guitar. He delighted in stating in his advance publicity that a wagon wheel had crushed his neck while he was a boy or that a fire had once seared his vocal cords or that a careless hunter's stray bullet had grazed his voice box—then recanting each tale from the stage, leaving his listeners intrigued and speculating about what had really happened.

Whatever the truth about the origin of Mickey Scarborough's unusual voice, there was one thing that was no mystery: It was a remarkably beautiful one, particularly when used to render the slow and sentimental ballads that Scarborough was famous for. When he sang of lonely orphans and doomed lovers and dying soldiers, even the staunchest and most rugged men would cry like babies. It was said that Ulysses S. Grant once grew so emotional upon hearing Scarborough's rendition of "Barbara Allen" that he had to leave the hall for fear of shaming himself.

Mickey Scarborough's Leadville performance, people would say for years thereafter, was the finest he ever gave. Those who had seen his earlier shows elsewhere claimed that his voice on that 1879 night was purer and higher than ever before, and far more emotion-filled. And that seemed particularly fitting, for after the Leadville performance, Scarborough never gave another. He died later than same night, leaving behind a legacy of excellent showmanship and a new mystery even greater than that of his warbling voice.

He collapsed on the stage, near the end of his show and at the close of a number so dramatic that some initially believed his trembling fall and astounding shout to be part of the performance. It happened like this: As the last chilling tenor note echoed away toward the mountain, Scarborough seemed to freeze in place, staring into the audience before him. His eyes grew wide and his face pale; then his hand rose, pointing into the crowd. He called a name loudly, twice, then fell to his knees, still pointing. A moment later, he gripped his chest, made a convulsive movement, and pitched straight forward, crushing his lute-shaped guitar to splinters beneath his heavy body.

For a few moments, the crowd stared in stunned silence, then with a collective cry surged forward and onto the stage, surrounding the fallen man. Someone rolled Scarborough onto his back; his eyes stared at the dark sky, and he whispered once more the name he had called, then dropped into unconsciousness. A local woman of means pushed through the crowd and to his side, examined him, then ordered that he be brought to her home for whatever care she could give him. A group of men carried Scarborough to a bed in her home, but her efforts came to nothing, for less than an hour later the Western Warblemaster was dead.

Scarborough's passing rocked all of Leadville, and not just because it was so shockingly dramatic in itself. Even more amazing was the name he had called. Witnesses to the collapse pounded each other with questions. "Did he say what I think he did?" "Yes," the answer would come, "not only called the name, but pointed out the very man attached to it there in the crowd, right there among us!" "Did you see who he pointed to?" "No, no I didn't—but surely someone did." "Scarborough must have seen the fellow himself, in the flesh, and gotten scared so badly by the sight that it killed him."

And so the rumors started, sweeping first through

Leadville, then through the surrounding countryside. The stage drivers carried the story with them into Fairplay, and from there on, it ran unfettered across Colorado, growing in the telling, stirring old feelings and furies, generating an explosive atmosphere in the town of Leadville that grew ever more volatile.

Mickey Scarborough could not have played out a more appropriately dramatic death scene had he been able to script it in advance. Nor could he have roused more awe and speculation if the name he had shouted in those moments before his passing had been that of Satan himself.

And so it all began. It was 1879, and the summer was edging toward fall.

# Chapter 1

He traveled in milling crowds, between rows of board-and-batten buildings, through relentless stenches and din. Above stretched a starry Colorado sky close enough to touch, below spread boot-sucking mud, and behind crept a one-armed man who had been Alex M. Gunnison's shadow for the last fifteen minutes.

Quickening his step, the young man pulled his sodden feet out of the mud and stepped onto the boardwalk where he cut around a pair of stumbling drunks and into the closest alley. He crossed a clay-slick miner passed out with his hand around his bottle, meandered through a maze of alleys, backlots, and sheds, then entered the middle of State Street, coming out beside a saloon band parked at the front door of its sponsoring establishment.

The band was drunk; it sometimes seemed half the people in this town were drunk, and proud of it. The four musicians were putting an old marching-band tune through a musical Inquisition, dismembering it in their brass torture chambers before spitting its remains into the night. Gunnison glanced behind him. His follower was gone.

Relieved, Gunnison began walking rapidly down

5

the State Street boardwalk. But he had forgotten the haphazard design of this town's walks and tripped when the low one he was on abruptly butted up against one a foot higher. It sent him sprawling. Immediately a man rushed to him, gave soothing words and a hand, and then was gone, taking with him Gunnison's wallet. Not that it mattered much. Gunnison had been wise enough to empty the cash from it last night in the dungeon of a hotel he had slept in, and now his fold of bills was stashed in his sock.

*All this is Brady Kenton's fault,* Gunnison thought bitterly as he brushed himself off. It was Kenton who had insisted on coming to Leadville for reasons unclarified; he who had walked happily down its dismal saloon-lined streets, exulting in the very smells and clamor that seemed so repelling to Gunnison; he who had vanished within two hours of their arrival yesterday afternoon, leaving his partner stranded like an abandoned orphan.

It wasn't the first time Kenton had done this to his companion. In Dodge City the previous summer, he had vanished for three days—difficult to do in a town that size, but Kenton had pulled it off. The prior spring in San Antonio he had given Gunnison the slip for a day. At least there had been plenty to enjoy in Dodge and San Antonio while searching him out. Gunnison's abandonments there had been mere temporary assignments to limbo. This one, though, was beginning to feel more like damnation to hell's outskirts.

Clumping glumly down the boardwalk, Gunnison had to scold himself for his overblown feelings. He knew he was not being fair to either Kenton or Leadville. Kenton didn't vanish simply to torment him. He did it because it was his way, and those ways, Gunnison was convinced, were largely beyond even Kenton's control. His modes of thinking and acting were written into his inimitable nature, as inerasable as an inscription on a gravestone, and there was nothing for Gunnison to do but live with them.

Kenton, who always preferred being addressed simply by his surname, was perhaps the most unusual man Alex Gunnison had ever known. Thoroughly Texan, sometimes brawlish, and uncomfortable without a Colt on his hip or beneath his coat, Kenton looked far more like a cattleman than like the journalistic chronicler he was. The look wasn't completely deceptive. Kenton had done some ranching in his day—that and a little of almost everything else. The man was an ongoing surprise to his younger friend and professional partner. Almost weekly, Gunnison discovered more about him and his wide-ranging experiences, and with every discovery held the man in a little more awe.

It was as a journalist that Gunnison knew Kenton best and admired him most. Wherever the chronicling team's travels took them, Kenton always managed to sniff his way, like a keen-nosed hound, into the heart of every place and time he chose to preserve in words and woodcuts. Too often, unfortunately, he sniffed his way into trouble as well, which was one of the reasons Gunnison's publisher father—Kenton's superior, if he could be said to have one—had assigned his son to travel and work with the unpredictable journalist.

Gunnison stopped and looked around. Where could Kenton be? Probably somewhere digesting the essence of this brawling Rocky Mountain silver camp ten thousand feet above the level of the distant ocean. Eventually, Gunnison knew, he would find Kenton, most likely with his pad filled with notes and sketch outlines that in finished form would enhance the pages of *Gunnison's Illustrated American* and prove once more that Brady Pleasant Kenton was the best of America's traveling artist-reporters.

Kenton was the idol of his counterparts at *Frank Leslie's Illustrated, Harper's Weekly,* and the like. Gunnison realized that many of them would gladly have traded places with him and become the one privileged to be Kenton's assistant and student—the second and more official capacity in which Gunnison traveled with him.

Winding through the crowd, Gunnison looked for Kenton's familiar form in the mix. Someone bumped him from the side; an artificial flowery smell rose into his nostrils, riding parasitically on the shoulders of a fleshy organic stench. An expanse of paint and powder slid sidewise across his line of vision; a yellow-toothed smile beamed.

"Well, ain't you the pretty one!" the powdered face said, exuding liquored breath. "Want to have a fine evening with Moll, my fine young dandy?"

"No, ma'am, no thank you." Gunnison backed away. Her perfume was overpowering, its putrid sweetness like rotting vegetables.

"Come with sweet Moll. You'll never forget it if you do."

"I'm sure I wouldn't, but no thank you all the same," Gunnison said. He tried to sidestep her, and her smile vanished. She stuck out her foot to make him stumble, but he dodged her. She swore at him, then swished on down the boardwalk trailing her smell like a wake. Within five seconds, she was accosting a new potential customer, this one inebriated enough to respond.

There, on down the street... Gunnison was sure he had seen Kenton. A tall, broad figure in the door of a gambling hall, there for a second and then gone....

Pushing through the crowd on the boardwalk proved frustratingly slow, so Gunnison descended to the muddy street again and there slogged a sticky path toward the gambling hall. He went to the door and looked around its packed interior. A haze of smoke he could have swum through dimmed the atmosphere, but a dozen hanging lamps pierced it sufficiently to show that Kenton was not there. The man Gunnison had seen was just one more of the thousands of miners and would-be miners who populated this town of unending flux.

Disappointed, Gunnison turned and started down the boardwalk again, passing an alley. Immediately a rough hand grabbed his collar. He yelled in surprise and was dragged back off the boardwalk into the alley where his head bumped hard against the gambling-house wall and he stared suddenly into eyes as dark and threatening as muzzle holes.

The eyes belonged to the one-armed man Gunnison thought he had evaded. He leaned close, the single hand gripping Gunnison's collar with the strength of two.

"Clean out your pockets! Clean 'em out now!" He punctuated the order with another firm rap of his victim's head against the wall, making sparks jump in his eyes. The man's breath was heavy with gin and the residue of opium smoke.

"I have nothing," Gunnison said.

"You're lying!" Another firm rap, more sparks inside his skull—but also a burst of anger. Gunnison remembered self-defense lessons forced on him in the past, with Kenton the eager teacher and Gunnison the reluctant student. Now he was glad for them. He swung his arm and knocked the grasping hand free, then drove up his knee, the man's groin the target. Gunnison missed, but his knee hit him at the base of his slightly overhanging belly. The fleshy mass absorbed the blow like a pillow.

Still, it hurt enough to make the man fall back. Gunnison dug beneath his vest for the small knife sheathed there. The three-inch blade glittered in the light from the street. Gunnison chuckled to see a flash of fear in the man's face. This one-armed devil would run from him now.

He didn't. Instead, he glared at Gunnison, breathing louder and faster as if he were trying to inflate himself. "Think to scare me off with that, do you?" he growled. Then another blade glittered, this one eight inches long and in the one-armed man's hand, not Gunnison's. It was the attacker's turn to chuckle. Gunnison's knife suddenly felt like a toy.

"Boy, you'd best find you a bucket to tote your bowels in!" The knife sliced toward Gunnison's abdomen and made him draw back. With a shudder of horror, Gunnison realized that the man was seriously trying to disembowel him. The man laughed again, advanced, and Gunnison lunged out blindly with his small blade.

The one-armed man yelped and drew back, his forearm bleeding, blood trickling to his elbow. Swearing, he came at Gunnison once more, his blade rising, then descending, flashing in reflected light as it speared toward Gunnison's midsection like sharp-edged lightning.

Gunnison was fully convinced he was about to die. There was no getting past this man and no avoiding his blade. Stiffening, he awaited the fatal thrust.

It did not come.

Instead there was a sudden flurry of motion and burst of noise. Before Gunnison could realize what had happened, his attacker was pinned against the wall, looking angrily into the face of a tall man with a mustache so thick it made his slender face look front-heavy. Balancing it somewhat was a brush of hair spilling down the back of his neck from beneath the brim of a Jefferson Davis hat that, like the man it was named after, had been beaten into submission long ago. The one-armed man's knife was now in the newcomer's hand.

"Chop-off Johnson, you leave this one alone, hear? I got business with him."

That comment suggested to Gunnison that maybe he was not going to escape robbery after all but simply fall victim to a two-armed bandit instead of a one-armed one.

The one-armed man scowled, then nodded reluctantly. "All right. For you, I'll do it, Currell. But give me back my knife."

The other nimbly flipped the knife and gave it, handle first, to its owner, a move about which Gunnison had very negative feelings.

"You had no call to jump me, Currell," Chop-off Johnson said. "You could have just hollered at me."

"Why, you'd have cut the tenderloins off him by then, Chop-off." Currell laughed and glanced at Gunnison, who didn't find the thought so amusing.

The one-armed man put away the knife and gave Gunnison the look of a hungry wolf deprived of a fresh kill. He turned and vanished into the dark.

Gunnison faced the other man. "Well, should I thank you or get ready to defend myself?"

"Don't fret. I ain't going to do nothing to you. Fact is, I been sent to find you, if you're Alex Gunnison."

Gunnison asked, "Did Brady Kenton send you?"

"That's right."

"Then I am Alex Gunnison."

"I thought so. Kenton said to look for a baby-faced fellow dressed like a swell."

He could have presented Gunnison no more convincing credentials than that last statement to verify that he had in fact been sent by Kenton. Gunnison's partner was a man of basics when it came to clothing. Though Gunnison's clothes were cut rugged and were hardly the fancy dress-coat outfits he had worn back in St. Louis, Kenton always perceived him as a dandified dresser. Gunnison had always put that down as one of Kenton's several blindnesses, but now he wasn't sure, for obviously Currell had perceived him in the same way.

Taking a deep breath, Gunnison let some of the tension of his encounter drain away. His muscles had petrified into a fist-sized knot between his shoulder blades. He nodded in the direction the one-armed man had run. "I appreciate the help. He had me a little worried."

"That was Maynard Johnson, Chop-off, we call him. He's an alleyway robber, what your locals call a footpad. He used to drive an ore wagon, like I do, until it rolled over his arm one day and they had to whack it off with nothing to cut the pain. Been sort of crazy-mad ever since, especially when he's drunk. But he barks more than he bites. Most days he's pretty normal, even works with me from time to time."

Gunnison put away his knife, and Currell thrust out his hand for a shake. "George Currell. Them who call me anything call me just plain Currell."

Currell's eyes were small, maybe brown, but black in this dim light. They flickered quickly up and down, and he smiled. "You're lucky you ain't been jumped before now, son. You got the look of the city about you. That don't slide down the local gullets too smooth, if you know what I mean."

"So I gather. Where is Kenton?"

"I'll take you to him. You got bags and such?"

"Yes, back at the hotel."

"Let's go get them. You've got a new place to sleep tonight, courtesy of Mr. Squire Deverell."

# Chapter 2

They retrieved his bag and the remainder of Kenton's baggage from the barnlike hotel Gunnison had slept in the previous night. Then Currell led him through town toward Kenton.

Gunnison sized up the man who had rescued him. Currell was built for power. Slender in waist and hip, from there up he was as stout as the big evergreens that towered over the squatty cabins on this part of East Third Street.

"What is it about driving an ore wagon that builds such muscle?" Gunnison asked.

"It's not the driving; it's the shoveling. I load my own wagon half the time," he said.

"You drive for a particular mine?"

"Any that will pay me, but mostly for Squire Deverell. Driving, building, general work—you know."

"Who is Squire Deverell?"

"Mine speculator who struck it rich. Well, not full rich, maybe, but well enough to show."

"So how'd you get the job of finding me?"

"Deverell heard Brady Kenton was in town and then happened to see him out his window. Recognized him from his picture in the *Illustrated American*. Deverell

13

likes Kenton's stories and pictures, and decided to help him out while he was in Leadville." Currell grinned. "And I figure he's hoping Kenton will do a story about him, but if you repeat that, I'll deny it. Anyway, Deverell had me go fetch Kenton off to some quarters he's got, and then they sent me to that hotel for you. You were gone, and I figured I wouldn't find you, but then I saw Chop-off working you over and said to myself: 'Currell, right there's your boy.' You're danged lucky I found you when I did. Chop-off might have made hash out of you and put your name in the papers. Speaking of papers, are you kin to the Gunnison who runs the *Illustrated American?*"

"My father."

"Well, how about that! I really like that paper. Especially them pictures. Does Kenton do all those?"

"I do about half, and half the writing too. But I don't get much of the credit."

"That's the way it usually goes in this old life, I've found."

They continued. Gunnison shifted his carpetbag in his hand, grateful he still possessed it. Since the morning, it had been entrusted, for a fee, to the care of the hotel keeper, and if that had been an uncertain option, it had seemed preferable to lugging the bag about all day in a town with more than its share of thieves. Luckily the keeper had made up in honesty what he lacked in hostmanship, and everything Gunnison left with him was intact when he picked it up.

Currell took lots of turns and shortcuts, and soon had Gunnison disoriented. In the end they came out on Harrison Avenue, a broad street, a finer-looking than most in Leadville and lined with restaurants, book and stationery shops, clothing shops, and liquor stores. They strode to a new building that was empty on the lower level but spilled orange light out of two upper windows.

Currell unlocked the street-level door and handed Gunnison the key. Opening with a clean squeak of new hinges, it admitted them into a dark building filled with the scent of fresh lumber.

"Deverell's going to open a hardware store in here in a few weeks," Currell said. "The upstairs is furnished out to live in. That's where you'll find your partner."

Light spilled out at the top of the stairway as a door opened. In it Kenton's familiar form was silhouetted. "Currell?" his voice boomed down. "Did you find my strayed pup?"

"Got him right here, Mr. Kenton."

Kenton dug into his pocket, produced an envelope, tossed it down. Despite the darkness, Currell deftly caught it.

"There's a difference between a strayed pup and an abandoned one, Kenton," Gunnison called up. "You deserted me, remember?"

"I guess I did at that, Alex. Anyway, you're back now, and I've got some drawings to show you. Currell, you come up and take a look too."

"Nope. Got to go." Currell touched his hat and spread his mustache in a sociable smile. He walked out, whistling, and closed the door behind him.

Kenton had already gone back inside the apartment. Gunnison plodded up the plank stairs, making a hollow echo in the empty store building.

Kenton had left the door ajar, and when Gunnison walked in, he was surprised by the pleasant furnishings. By big-city standards, this was no fancy place; by Gunnison's, after the previous night's suffering, it was luxurious. The walls were crisp white, the floor varnished to a sheen. The furniture included overstuffed chairs, a sturdy table, a sofa, and a big iron stove for heat and cooking. At the end of the room, a door led into a kitchen, and another opened onto a short hallway, beyond which he saw the doors of what were probably two bedrooms.

"Good to have you back safe and sound, Alex," Kenton said without looking up. He had a pencil behind his ear and another in his hand, and was leaning over the collapsible drawing board that he had designed and custom-built. He was sketching a saloon scene.

Gunnison slammed down the bags. "Don't pretend you were worried about me, Kenton. You didn't waste two thoughts on me, and you know it."

Kenton looked up, heavy brows lifting over green eyes framed with wrinkles. His frameless spectacles, worn only when he was working, rode low on his long nose, their sidepieces losing themselves in his graying sideburns. Hair of the same hue shagged down on the sides, flattened above Kenton's ears by a full day's pressure from the band of the cattleman's hat he always wore. His face was tanned and roughly whiskered, for Kenton generally lacked the patience for a careful shaving job. Snaking out of his left sideburn nearly to the tip of his wide mustache was a long slash scar—a memento of his wartime years. His intense eyes glittered in the light of the twin lamps poised on the flat upper edge of his drawing board.

Kenton took a long breath and exhaled as if to signal that Gunnison's aggravation was unwarranted. "I had some private business to see to," he said in his sleepy drawl, "and I didn't figure you for some runt who can't get by on his own for a while. But I reckon I do make it hard for you to do a proper job of riding herd on me like your pap wants. Maybe you ought to abandon me. Go off and marry Glorietta Sweat, and rescue her from that last name of hers."

Gunnison didn't like it when Kenton made fun of his fiancée's name. So he shot back, "Yes, Pleasant. Perhaps I should do that."

Kenton's brow rose, and his mustache twitched. He despised being called by his middle name, the maiden name of his mother. Gunnison gigged him with it only when Kenton made fun of Glorietta Sweat.

Gunnison picked up his bag and went back to one of the bedrooms, which proved to be as nicely furnished as the main room.

"Currell said this place has been loaned to us," Gunnison called out to Kenton.

"That's right. We seem to have found ourselves a friend named Squire Deverell. We're supposed to go meet him in the morning." Kenton's pencil scratched out the familiar rhythm of his signature, marking one more finished sketch. "Well, there's another one branded and ready to turn loose. Come in here, Alex—tell me what you think."

Gunnison walked over and inspected the drawing. "Very good," he said. "Wonderful detail." And indeed it was. There in one corner was an image of Chop-off Johnson accurate enough to make Gunnison shudder.

Kenton yawned, adjusted the lamps, and set to work on a new sketch, working from a small crude one on his pocket pad.

Gunnison sighed quietly and decided to forget his irritation at Kenton. Pardoning the man's ways was a skill Gunnison had mastered long ago, for Kenton had provided lots of opportunities for practice. Gunnison was getting so good at forgiving that sometimes he sardonically wondered if he should enter the priesthood.

Returning to his room, Gunnison went to bed, rolled over, and closed his eyes. It felt marvelous, and the covers were warm, but the noise of Leadville seeped through the walls like water through paper, disturbing him. Besides that, he couldn't get the image of Chop-off Johnson's glittering knife out of his mind. Sleep would take a long while to come tonight.

# Chapter 3

As he lay restlessly in his room in Leadville, nostrils filled with the fresh wood scent of the new walls and ears filled with the ruckus of the streets beyond them, Alex Gunnison found himself reliving the somewhat bewildering chain of events that had brought him and Brady Kenton to this remarkable town.

The two journalists had been in the midst of a tour of Colorado's cattle ranches, large and small, their goal a colorful description and depiction of that growing business for the readers of the *Illustrated American*. Alex found the work fascinating but tiring; at length even the unwearying Kenton seemed eager for a rest, and marked off a Saturday afternoon for a time of leisure.

In the cool luxury of Colorado Springs's El Paso Club they relaxed, letting their thoughts flow slowly and freely. Tall cool drinks chilled their hands, and the soft cushions of padded chairs made of finely crafted, scroll-topped wood rested their tired backs. The afternoon was waning slowly, lazy seconds ticking off one by one on a beautiful oaken clock replete with carved flamingoes and hung on a wall of sage-green paper. Kenton was reading a cheap novel, as he often did to relax; Gunnison was half dozing, glad to be away from the heat and dust of the cattle ranches. A fly buzzed about in the open window that he faced, making droning, lulling music. Through slowly drooping eyelids Gunnison was gazing through that window at a splendid view of Cheyenne Mountain when he was roused by the opening of the door. One of the El Paso Club employees entered and approached Kenton, letter in hand.

"Delivered only moments ago, sir," the letter bearer said in what sounded to Gunnison like a poorly faked British accent.

Kenton twitched his broad mustache. "Thank you," he said.

Kenton began to open the letter. The deliverer remained at his side. When Kenton looked up at him inquiringly, the man smiled and gave a little waggle of his right hand in a none-too-subtle request for a gratuity. Kenton frowned, but the glare in his eyes was almost immediately replaced by a twinkle. Kenton placed his hand into the man's and pumped vigorously. "Thank you again, sir, and God save the king," he said.

The letter bearer's face went dark. "Good afternoon to you, sir," he said, this time with more South Carolina than Yorkshire in his inflection. He turned on his heel and stalked out.

Kenton finished opening the letter and read silently. When he was done, he gave his mouth a wry twist, raised one brow, and began folding the letter back into the envelope. Gunnison was surprised to see he looked a little pale.

"Is something wrong, Kenton?"

Kenton glanced at him. "No, no. It's from Victor Starlin... I've often wondered whatever happened to him. Haven't heard from him in years."

"Starlin? Sounds familiar."

"I've mentioned him to you sometime or other, probably. We served together back in the hostilities."

"So where is he now?"

"Herding sheep right here in El Paso County. Sheep! It's not something I would have figured him to ever do. It's a surprise to hear from him."

"How did he know you were here?"

"He tracked us down by telegraphing the St. Louis office. He wants very badly for me to come see him."

"Will I be going along?"

"In this case, perhaps you better stay here and finish up some of those sketches you've started."

"Oh." Gunnison was not eager to work in dull isolation while Kenton was off seeing new and interesting things.

His disappointment must have been detectable in his tone because Kenton looked closely at him. "Oh, hang it all," he said resignedly, "Come along if you want."

Gunnison was pleased. "Thanks. I've always been interested in sheepherders. It's an isolated life they live."

Kenton did not respond. He was staring solemnly at the envelope, deep in thought, his brow furrowed.

"Kenton, are you sure everything is all right?"

"Of course it is, Alex."

That night as he prepared to go to bed, Gunnison saw Kenton seated in the corner of his own room, the letter open again and lying on the foot of his bed as Kenton cleaned his pistol.

The following morning, the two of them put on their stoutest riding clothes, rented horses at a stable, and set out for Austin's Bluffs, five miles to the northwest. Their sketch pads and pencils were tucked into saddlebags; their pistols were stashed in their holsters.

A more beautiful ride Gunnison had never experienced. The day was clear and slightly brisk despite the season, and their horses traveled well. Looming to the west were mountains that reached so far into the sky, it seemed they would pierce the floor of heaven. Sky and mountain, together with the wind sweeping across the wild land, created an aura of vastness that was both thrilling and humbling. This was an awesome place, a place where a man might hear distant rolls of thunder from the mountains and for a moment wonder if the rumbling booms were really the footfalls of God himself striding across his own spectacular creation just for the pleasure of it.

So undiminished was today's view that looking south, the riders could see not only the Sierra Mojada, but also the Spanish Peaks. Gunnison had always loved mountains, particularly the Rockies, and today he was so overcome with their stony beauty that he was all but oblivious to everything else around him. Even Kenton might have been forgotten had he not been singing in his rough but listenable baritone, his voice unfurling across the Colorado countryside. The song was some sort of Texas funeral dirge, but the bright sunlight and the vigor of Kenton's singing took all the sorrow out of it and made it almost sprightly.

El Paso County was sheep country; within its borders as many as two hundred thousand sheep roamed, grazing on the hills and meadows, surviving remarkably fierce winters. Public lands here could be bought from the government at auctions, the highest bidder winning out, or at a dollar twenty-five an acre. Land could be taken by "preemption," or through occupation for five years under terms of the Homestead Law. Alternatively, land scrip could be purchased, this scrip representing unclaimed lands offered by the government to Union veterans of the civil conflict. Kenton had explained all these things to Gunnison as they rode out of Colorado Springs. The man was a deep well of such information; he absorbed facts as sand absorbs water. The sheep business, Kenton told Gunnison, was hated by cattle-men, but the fact remained that a man could make good money at it if he could endure the accompanying loneliness and rigors.

Victor Starlin's letter apparently included direc-tions to his ranch, for Kenton consulted it often, complaining about Starlin's poor penmanship as he struggled to decipher parts of it. Gunnison offered to help him, but was refused quickly and firmly. Gunnison had noticed how little his partner had told him of the letter's content and recalled that Kenton initially had planned to make this journey alone. Obviously Starlin had written something Kenton did not want him to know about—and Gunnison set himself in expectation of being sent away from the ranch, probably on some journalistic pretext, so the men could talk alone. His curiosity began to rise about that mysterious letter.

At length they reached the head of a little valley that was overgrown with a yellow-tinged grass and almost entirely lacking trees, and in it saw the sheep ranch of Victor Starlin. There was nothing ostentatious about the ranch: a little double cabin, roughly but sturdily built to survive the heavy snowfalls that sometimes literally buried entire flocks. Sheep corrals were all about the cabin, connected by narrow gated chutes. A smattering of outbuildings stood here and there, and behind the cabin ran a spring. There was no sign of life about the place other than a tiny trickle of smoke rising from the chimney to the sky, coming, he expected, from the remnant coals of the morning's breakfast fire.

"We may be in for a wait until near nightfall," Kenton said. "Victor is probably out with his flocks."

No sooner were the words said, however, than

around the back of the farthest shed came a lean booted
man wearing a Mexican-style hat and a long lightweight
canvas coat. He stopped when he saw the newcomers,
pushed up the face-shadowing brim of the hat, looked
them over carefully, then waved his hand and started
toward them at a trot.

"Victor Starlin?"

"Yes indeed," Kenton replied. "A sight to see for
these tired old eyes."

He smiled broadly, raised his hand over his head,
and waved back at Starlin, and the pair began their
descent into the shepherd's valley.

# Chapter 4

Starlin served his coffee so hot that the heat came right through the handles of the battered tin cups the men held and obliged them to rest them on the splintery tabletop, lifting them only long enough to take quick and careful sips before putting them down again.

Victor Starlin was a young-looking man despite the gray around his temples; it was difficult to picture him and Kenton as contemporaries from the war years. But contemporaries they were, and they shared half-told stories and inside jokes that they obviously found very amusing but to Gunnison were indecipherable.

Gunnison sat, a quiet listener, hoping they would forget him and talk freely about the mysterious matter upon which Kenton had been summoned and their war experiences. Despite his Texas heritage, Kenton had been active for the Union in the war, yet he had never described his activities to Gunnison or even his exact military affiliations. All Gunnison had been able to surmise was that Kenton had been involved in some sort of dangerous intelligence work, that he had served far from home and had come close to death several times.

If Starlin was a wartime cohort, he had likely been

involved in the same things, but Gunnison's hopes to learn what those were proved as vain with Starlin as they had with Kenton. Starlin chose his words carefully and betrayed little of himself and his past.

The evening came, and the flocks returned, Starlin's hired Mexican shepherds with them. By the time the sheep were corralled and the workers were inside, Starlin had already cooked up a fine-smelling pot of beans, an ovenload of aromatic mutton, and three excellent loaves of bread.

"My cook quit me a week ago," he said. "Since then, I've given up the fields and taken to the kitchen.

"And a fine kitchen maid you make," Kenton said. "This is prime. You'd find no finer food or shelter in many a town."

In Gunnison's view, Kenton was right about the food but lying about the shelter. The men were seated around the smallish table, badly crowded and bumping elbows on all sides. Starlin's shepherds, Mexicans to the last man, were big in their movements and loud in their eating, and put on quite a show as they downed the food. Watching the vigorous way the sated their appetites was almost enough to take away Gunnison's. By the time the meal was ended, their beards were soaked in grease, gravy, and the juice of cooked beans. There was nothing Mexican about Starlin's cooking, but that didn't seem to bother the shepherds.

Kenton, always one to join in the spirit of things, had eaten with equal vigor and had splattered a varied pattern of stains down the front of his shirt. Gunnison mentally faulted his partner for sloppiness until he glanced at his own shirt and saw he had done the same thing, because of the jostling of his tablemates.

Kenton and Gunnison bedded down on the floor that night, sleeping well despite the all-night snores around them. As Gunnison dozed off, he realized that he still had not learned why Kenton had been called here in that secretive fashion.

The next morning, they were up before dawn and at their breakfast as the first sunrays shone in from the direction of Kansas. This would be the time, Gunnison expected, that Kenton would find a way to be rid of him so that he could talk to Starlin without a listener.

His expectation proved correct. Kenton informed Gunnison that Gunnison was to be a shepherd for a day, going out with one of the Mexicans to watch over the flock—though his main job would be sketching, not shepherding.

"Are you coming?" Gunnison asked.

"No, no—I think our purpose would be best served for me to stay here and discuss the business end of the sheep enterprise with Victor. You go on alone."

Though he was frustrated at being denied knowledge of what Victor and Kenton were to discuss, the day proved interesting. The name of the shepherd with whom Gunnison went was Juan Cortez, and though he spoke poor English, he had a way of making himself clear through gestures and symbols when speech failed him.

As the day passed, Cortez described his life and routine. He told of the hardships and pleasures of shepherding—the pleasures being the time it allowed him for a solitude that he usually loved (having been raised in a two-room house with twelve brothers and sisters) and the possibility of building up a flock of his own, for Starlin paid him partly in lambs. The hardships were the occasional loneliness and most of all, the snowstorms.

Cortez told him of times he had dug sheep from beneath ten feet of snow in which they had been imprisoned for up to three weeks and seen them survive, having burrowed down through the snow to the sparse winter grass. He talked of the icy winds that sliced through the heaviest of coverings and chilled a man to the marrow and the dangers of becoming lost with an entire flock when a sudden blizzard struck. In a prior year, he said, a terrible storm had struck the region, leading to tragedy in a gulch near Colorado Springs. In the Big Corral area, more than a thousand sheep wandered over the edge of a bluff unseen in the storm and died below, piled atop each other in the snow. What was worse, their shepherd died right along with them; he was a Mexican, and an acquaintance of Cortez's. Such tragedies were simply part of the hazardous life of the Colorado sheepherder.

Cortez was an easy fellow to like, and he seemed very intelligent. Toward the end of the day, it struck Gunnison that the shepherd might have some knowledge of what it was that Victor Starlin wanted with Kenton beyond the renewal of old friendship. Gunnison asked him about it, trying to be casual and subtle.

At the question, Cortez's dark eyes narrowed, and he looked around as if to make sure they were not being watched, even though the nearest human beings were surely at least a mile away. Into Gunnison's ear he whispered a word that the journalist did not understand because of Cortez's accent.

"I beg your pardon?" he said.

He repeated it; this time it was a little more clear and sounded like "Garrote."

"What do you mean?"

"Garote!" he repeated. "Garote! Garrote!" He put his hand to his throat and thrust out his tongue in imitation of choking.

"Oh, yes," said Gunnison. "I see."

In fact, he did not see at all. Victor Starlin was afraid of being garroted, and so he called Brady Kenton to come see him? It made no sense, but pride made Gunnison unwilling to admit his confusion.

The evening found Gunnison and Cortez on their way back to the corrals. As instructed, Gunnison had completed a padful of rough sketches that could later be finished out. Kenton would be pleased, he hoped. But when he tried to show Kenton his work, the man did not seem interested. He was greatly distracted. Whatever Starlin had told him today about this indecipherable "garrote" matter must have been intriguing.

"Did you have a productive day with Mr. Starlin?" Gunnison asked Kenton when they had a private moment.

"Yes, indeed," he said.

"Well, I suppose it's back to the cattle ranches for us now."

"Hmmm? Oh, yes, but not for long. We've got another thing to do just as quick as we can get to it. We'll finish out our work around Pueblo, then head out."

"Where?"

"Up, into the mountains. We're going to Leadville."

# Chapter 5

And that was how they had come to Leadville: Kenton determined to get there at all due speed, Gunnison uncertain why they were going at all. When Gunnison pressed Kenton about it, he received only a declaration that the journey was being undertaken out of journalistic interest, nothing more.

"But," Gunnison objected, "we're in the middle of a ranch tour, and Leadville is a mining town."

Kenton responded with the sort of patient-but-weary tone that a parent would use with an over-inquisitive child. Leadville, he explained was one of the most newsmaking towns in the nation, with every would-be miner on the continent making for it. Two railroads had engaged in an unprecedented armed war over a right-of-way to reach it, involving even the well-known Kansas peace officer Bat Masterson. Every American had the name Leadville on the tip of his tongue. They could hardly afford to pass it by.

Gunnison wasn't inclined to argue with Kenton, having long before learned the futility of that, but he did not accept Kenton's explanation. Something Victor Starlin had told him was behind this—and it was all the more intriguing in that Kenton clearly didn't want Gunnison to know what it was.

As they departed Austin's Bluffs, Starlin approached Kenton, who was already saddled. "If you need any assistance in Leadville, look up a cousin of mine who is there. His name is Percival Starlin, but he goes by 'Perk' for short. He's a simple and shiftless sort of fellow, but true to the bone in a tight spot, and knows what goes on in that town. I've already sent him a letter saying you'd likely be coming."

"I'll keep him in mind. Thanks for the hospitality, Victor."

The riders returned to Colorado Springs and settled their affairs and accounts, then headed south toward Pueblo to fulfill their appointment. That ate up an entire day, during which Kenton's restlessness to head for Leadville was increasingly evident.

When at last they were done, they boarded the Rio Grande Railroad and wound up, by merit of Kenton's unique mix of charm and pushiness, riding for several miles in the cab with the engineer. Kenton sketched and interviewed him simultaneously, and Gunnison took notes in the background as they rambled along a smoke-belching route through the mountains.

At track's end they left the train and caught one of several Leadville stages, and it was here Gunnison's experience began to go sour. The journalists were packed in like tinned fish with six other passengers, several of whom seemed to be all knees and elbows. Kenton, in typical good fortune, found his seat beside a lovely young blonde of about twenty. Once he told her who he was, she was obviously enthralled to find herself in the company of so famous a journalist. Her big doe eyes remained on Kenton for most of the journey, absorbing every gesture as he regaled her with stories of his exploits—many embellished and a few outright fiction-

al. As for Gunnison, he was across the coach, squeezed
in misery between the girl's fat mother and a flatulent
drummer for whose indiscretions he sensed he was
receiving general blame.

The stagecoach came at last to the foot of Mosquito
Pass, the final barrier between them and Leadville. A
new road lay ahead, and the coach began a torturous
ascent toward a summit of more than thirteen thousand
feet. The vehicle creaked and groaned; the fat woman
shifted, grinding Gunnison's side like a millstone. The
driver outside swore a lot, loudly, and drove with
obvious nervousness.

As they climbed, the temperature dropped, and
for every fallen degree, the girl shifted a little closer to
Kenton. Outside, a fast-descending fog obliterated the
peaks. Coneys and rabbits by the dozens scampered
over the rocks, frightened by the clatter and creak of
the stage. The coach scraped over stumps, banged
through ruts, moved through the murk like a ghost ship
on a misty ocean.

At last the travelers crossed the crest and descended
toward Leadville, which lay in a valley surrounded by
hills from which much vegetation had been stripped,
making parts of the region look strangely blasted against
the splendid mountain backdrop. Heavy lines of black
and yellow smoke rose above the town, belched out by
smelters.

The stage swung onto Chestnut Street, the oldest
avenue in the town, and rode between rows of typical
Western buildings. Some were ornamented brick structures, others smaller wooden false fronts, still others
mere glorified sheds with canvas roofs.

The stage creaked to a halt. People were everywhere—
walking, riding, building, laughing, arguing on the
boardwalks and trash-strewn streets. The bustle rivaled
New York's. That was no surprise; newcomers were

arriving in Leadville at the reported rate of a hundred or more a day. Kenton predicted they would have trouble finding quarters.

He was right. After departing the stage—Kenton bowed and tipped his hat in farewell to the young lady and her mother, leaving both staring wistfully after him—they strode together through the streets, carrying their bags and Kenton's folded drawing table, vainly trying to find lodging. They finally checked into what purported to be a hotel; thereafter, Kenton vanished, and Gunnison was left to wander alone through the course of events that led him ultimately to a State Street alley, the frightening attack by Chop-off Johnson, and his providential rescue by George Currell.

When Gunnison's remembrances faded enough finally to let him go to sleep, two men walked through the alley below his window, arguing loudly. Both sounded agitated and drunk. Their voices faded as they moved past, and a momentary lull followed during which Gunnison heard Kenton's snore from the main room where he had been working.

Rising, Gunnison found Kenton slumped over his drawing table, asleep. His cheek rested against a half-finished drawing; rejected ones lay crumpled and scattered on the floor around his chair, finished ones in a neat stack nearby. One of the lamps on his drawing table had burned itself out, and the other was barely flickering. Between them stood an amber whiskey bottle, open, and a shot glass with half a swallow remaining.

It saddened Gunnison when Kenton drank over his work, for it always indicated he was thinking again of his lost Victoria, dead now for twenty years, the victim of some accident Kenton had never described. The nature and circumstances of her death were just one more of the several secrets Kenton held closely.

Gunnison walked to the drawing table and cranked up the lamp that still burned. Kneeling beside the pile of completed sketches, he picked up one depicting a crowd on Chestnut Avenue. Scanning it, he found what he knew he would.

Victoria Kenton, recognizable to him because he had often seen the tiny oil portrait of her that Kenton kept with him, looked out on the penciled-in street from a third-story window, barely noticeable if one was not specifically looking for her. Her subtle image turned up often in Kenton's work, particularly when he most missed her.

Gunnison put down the sketch and blew out the lamp, then went back to bed to wait for morning.

# Chapter 6

Kenton's baritone boomed through the apartment. Sitting up and rubbing the back of his petrified neck, Gunnison wondered how his fifty-year-old partner could sound so vigorous after a night spent slumped stiffly over a drawing table.

He pulled on his clothes and stumbled out of his room. Kenton was in his own room splashing steaming water from a washstand bowl across his face. Mumbling a good morning, Gunnison went to the stove where Kenton had warmed a kettle and poured a pitcherful for his own washup. Fifteen minutes later, both Kenton and he were dressed and ready to begin their day— though Gunnison still remained unsure just what they had come to do.

On the street the air was bitingly fresh, and a cool wind whipped down from Mount Zion. Gunnison checked his watch—only half past seven, and already the town was as busy as if it were noon.

Kenton had just declared a taste for a flapjack breakfast when a scratching noise caught their attention. A young man crouched at the front of a saloon about two doors down was digging for change in the spittle-permeated sawdust that had been swept out a little earlier.

Kenton strode over to him. "Young fellow, could you steer two hungry men toward a couple of stacks of Leadville's best flapjacks?"

Blue eyes reconnoitered Kenton's form. "I know you—you're Brady Kenton!" the boy declared in a light Irish brogue. "I heard talk you were in town. My father, he always read your stories."

Kenton appreciated recognition even from a mining-town street boy. Ever since the *Illustrated American*'s decision to place a woodcut portrait of its best-known writer-artist in the nameplate, Kenton was recognized everywhere he went. Often he complained about the heavy burden of fame, but Gunnison knew better. Kenton loved the attention.

"I am Brady Kenton," he said. "And who are you?"

"My name's Lundy O'Donovan," the boy said. He looked about twelve, was destined for lankiness, and had sandy chopped-off hair that reminded Gunnison of a mown wheat field. His big teeth, yellow despite his youth, were rooted in a prominent jaw as Irish as his name.

"Pleased to know you, Lundy." Kenton introduced Gunnison and asked Lundy again about flapjacks.

"Go to French John's on Harrison. They make hotcakes good as my mother's."

"Thank you, son," said Kenton. He waved toward the pile of outsweepings. "Tell me, have you had much luck prospecting that sawdust?"

"Not so far."

"Have yourself a grubstake, then." Kenton dug in his pocket and brought out a coin for the boy, who accepted it with delight.

They found the restaurant and ordered a big meal.

As they ate, Gunnison described his encounter with Chop-off Johnson, which horrified Kenton and seemed to make him honestly repentant about deserting his partner for so long. What with the satisfaction that brought, plus a heap of flapjacks tucked comfortably under his belt, Gunnison decided Leadville wasn't so bad, after all, despite his rough start here. Leaning back in his chair, he enjoyed a final cup of coffee before Kenton dabbed his lips with a checkered napkin and declared it was time to go.

The morning light was brighter and richer now. The air had gone a little foul, though; a smell of garbage floated on the breeze, sweeping in from somewhere on the edge of town. They explored Harrison Avenue, then headed down State Street. On the latter Gunnison showed Kenton where he had been attacked by Johnson outside the gambling hall.

But Kenton was looking the other way. "Tell me, Alex, isn't that sprout getting such a bad time yonder the same one who steered us to the café?"

He pointed across the street toward an alleyway where, sure enough, Lundy O'Donovan was being shaken and slapped by a much bigger boy. Two other boys loitered behind the abuser, grinning at the show.

A moment later Kenton was stomping across the street. Gunnison fell in behind. The boy doing the slapping turned as they approached. Upon seeing Kenton's tall figure bearing down on him, his eyes grew big, and he blanched. But in another moment he had pasted on a sneer.

"This young man happens to be a friend of mine," Kenton said. "I suggest you leave him alone unless you want a three-day headache."

The boy called Kenton a "boar's rump" and speculated on his parentage. Kenton stretched out his big hands and grabbed the offender at the base of the neck.

The youth tried to slap the hands away but found he could not lift his arm to do it, for Kenton had pinched a nerve. Gunnison had seen him do this trick before. Kenton had tried to teach it to him, but he had never been able to pick it up.

The boy gave a loud, shuddering moan and screwed up his face in pain. His two companions looked horrified, turned, and ran away.

"You're sorry, I suppose?" Kenton asked.

"Yes! Yes! I'm sorry!"

"You sure about that? Really sure?"

"Yes! I'm sure! I'm sure!"

Kenton released his victim, who slid to his heels, shuddered, bounced up, and ran off.

Kenton shifted his attention to Lundy. "Are you all right, partner?"

"I am now, thanks to you, Mr. Kenton." Lundy beamed at his rescuer with adoration.

"Were they after money?"

"Yes. But I didn't give it to them."

"Good. Now, you keep away from them for a time, Lundy. They'll be prone to give you trouble if they find you alone."

"I ain't scared of them," Lundy said.

They walked away. A block later, Gunnison whispered, "Kenton, he's following us."

"I know. We don't need a tagalong, but I hate to outright tell him to go away." He waved toward a mining-goods store to their right. "Let's duck in here for a moment and see if that breaks him off."

The store smelled of leather, metal, and tobacco. They examined its inventory a few minutes, then Gunnison went back to the door and stepped out. No Lundy on the street.

"Mister?"

The boy had parked himself in a squat by the door,

obviously waiting for the journalists to emerge. Gunnison hadn't seen him when he came out.

"Lundy, are you following us?"

"Yes, sir. I've thought of a way I can repay you for your help back there."

"Thanks, Lundy, but there's no need."

"But I know about something you'll want to draw up for your newspaper. Something really secret, all about Briggs Garrett."

Gunnison smiled. Lundy obviously had an active imagination. Garrett, a hated Confederate night-rider leader whose main claim to infamy was the brutal hanging and burning of Unionist bridge burners in eastern Tennessee during the Civil War, had been officially listed as accidentally killed two years before. He had washed away in a flood and reportedly drowned. The *Illustrated American* itself had carried a story about it.

"When we decide to search for ghosts, we'll be sure to check with you," Gunnison said.

Lundy's smile remained bright. "He's no ghost. Ain't you heard all the talk? He's alive and right here in Leadville—there was a singer here who saw him right from the stage!" Now Lundy took on a cunning look. "Everybody's been talking about it, but I can prove it's true. I'll come around later and show you what I mean. I saw where you're staying. Bye now!" He turned and ran down the middle of the street, waving over his shoulder as he disappeared into the milling crowds of Leadville.

Kenton joined Gunnison at the door. "What did he want?"

"Nothing that matters. Just some childish nonsense."

"Quite a little fire spitter," Kenton said. "I like that boy, somehow. Persistent, you know. Lives his own life and does what he wants. I was a lot like him when I was that age."

"You haven't changed."

Kenton gave a wry smile. "Come on," he said. "We got us a duty call to pay on Mr. Squire Deverell."

# Chapter 7

The journalists quickly discovered, as Kenton would say sometime later, that Squire Deverell "had more bile packed in his gullet than you could render out of a wagonload of bad livers." What was worse, he was eager to share it.

Kenton and Gunnison sat in their benefactor's parlor, sketching and recording Deverell as he alternated between describing his trek to fortune and expounding upon his many hatreds. Currell had been right; it was obvious Deverell assumed the journalists owed him inclusion in the *Illustrated American* in return for their free lodging.

Deverell had come from Denver two years before and opened a clothing and dry goods store in Leadville, he said. From that base he had begun grubstaking miners. His gambles had paid off to the point that he sold his store and now spent all his time in mine speculation. His earnings, he admitted, were not enough to put him among Colorado's elite yet, but were at least sufficient to bring him a well-off status and an impressive house.

At the moment he was pacing back and forth before that house's most extravagant feature: a fireplace big enough to spit-roast a bison in. Deverell was a fascinating figure to his visitors, though in an unpleasant way. He had a head as round as a cannonball, slick-bald on the top but fringed around the ears with unruly white hair. The back of his neck was covered with a pale thin fuzz that caught light like spider silk when he turned at certain angles; Kenton was doing his best to capture that phemonenon on his sketch pad. He wore a black silk house robe over maroon trousers and a shirt of vomitous yellow-green. If the combination was unnerving, it was eye-catching.

As Kenton sketched, Gunnison took notes of Deverell's diatribes. Nothing the man had to say was worthy of the pages of the *Illustrated American*, but they felt obliged to humor him with an interview. By the time he found out no story would result, they would be long gone from Leadville.

Deverell hated everyone, from Swedes to Chinamen to Irishmen to Negroes to Jews to Catholics to lawyers. On two points he tempered his bigotry a little; he acknowledged that Irishmen had developed two of his most productive claims and lawyers had helped him retain them through a complicated legal dispute. Beyond that, he had nothing good to say about anyone.

Deverell turned to a large wall map upon which local mining claims had been faithfully penciled in, ones he held an interest in being outlined in blue. Abundant erasures on the map showed that the man followed the flux of changing mining claims in the compulsive way others follow every development in the stock market or at the betting track.

"Look at it, gentlemen—a maze of overlapping claims. A puzzle thrown out of a box with all the pieces landing atop each other. Paradise for lawyers and hell for the rest. I despise lawyers. I'd rather marry my daughter to a one-legged Chinaman as to trust a nickel and the time of day to a lawyer. Don't you agree, Mr. Kenton?"

"Not having a daughter, I don't feel qualified to hold an opinion," Kenton said with a smile.

Deverell looked irritated. "I don't have a daughter either, sir. It was just a figure of speech to make a point. What I was trying to get across was—"

He cut off as into the room came his remarkably pleasant little wife, her smile etched across a thin face scrimshawed with wrinkles. She bustled in with far more tea and cookies than the journalists' recent flapjack breakfast could let them comfortably consume. Kenton figured her for one of those good women God sometimes gave to rotten men to sweeten them a little, like sugar in bitter coffee.

Kenton praised the cookies and made her blush so that the wrinkles stood out like the lines on her husband's map. After she returned to the kitchen, Deverell looked sadly after her, leaned forward, and whispered: "Don't let the wrinkles make you think Mary's old. Those are the result of a patent face cream sold to her by a drummer who swore it would make her skin like a baby's. I sued him for all he was worth, which was too little in any case, and didn't even get a cent of that. Lawyers again."

Something bumped a window to their left, and a figure ascended diagonally outside it on a staircase that ran up the outside of the house past the window. It was George Currell. He glanced in and touched his hat in greeting, a somber expression on his face. Kenton nodded back. In a moment they heard footsteps bumping around above.

"I didn't notice a third floor from the outside," Kenton said, for they were on the second level.

"There isn't a complete floor, just some rooms on one end. Mark Straker, Mary's nephew, lives there."

Deverell said the word "nephew" as if he were mouthing a green persimmon.

"How did he come to live with you?" Kenton was glad to have a chance to shift the subject away from Deverell's menu of prejudices.

"His mother was Mary's sister; she died of fever. His father was killed at Gettysburg. Mary and I raised him—Mary absolutely adores him." He paused. "I wish I could feel the same toward him. Mark turned out . . . harsh. I have never understood why."

Kenton could have ventured a likely guess, but prudence made him keep his mouth shut.

Deverell, who for a second had dropped his pompous front to reveal a more human aspect, said nothing for several moments, looking out the window. As he did so, Currell descended again, accompanied by a young man whose handsome features were marred only by unusually dark rings beneath his eyes, marking him as a habitual reveler. Clearly this was Mark Straker. Straker was slipping on a coat as he descended the stairs; beneath it he wore a Remington pistol, high and butt forward.

Kenton rose. "Mr. Deverell, I'm afraid we have to leave you for now. Deadlines and other work to do, you know. Thank you so much for all you've done for us."

Deverell looked displeased to see his audience about to bolt for freedom so soon. "Mr. Kenton, I hoped to hear from you about your California tour of seventy-five."

Kenton felt a slight stab of embarrassment, as he always did when that subject was brought up in front of Gunnison. Deverell was referring to a celebrated series of stories and drawings Kenton had done four years before in a tour of the West Coast. Kenton, always prone to find trouble, had been even more so in those days before he had begun cutting back on his drinking.

The California tour, though a brilliant journalistic success, had brought the *Illustrated American* a spate of bills deriving from various saloon brawls and the like. One bill was for $578 for damage to a saloon devastated by Kenton in a brawl he couldn't even remember.

The "unfortunate incident on the western coast," as J. B. Gunnison, publisher of the *Illustrated American* and father of Alex, had come to call the California tour, was what had resulted in the assignment of Alex Gunnison as Kenton's apprentice.

Kenton made a habit of complaining about having been assigned a watchdog. In the beginning, the complaints had been sincere, but gradually he had grown fond of his young partner. The gripes had lost their sincerity, though Kenton still carried them on for the sake of banter and habit. Kenton had a deep affection for Gunnison, though he sometimes wondered if the young fellow would ever open his eyes wide enough to become the prime chronicler he could be.

To Deverell Kenton said, "I'd love to tell you about the California tour, but duty calls, and we need to sketch while the light is best."

"You're going to put what I've said in your paper, I hope?"

"I have a specific place in mind for everything you've given us."

He glanced at Gunnison, who grinned covertly back at him. Gunnison knew what the comment meant, but Deverell took it as a yes and looked happy. He suggested that Kenton and Gunnison rejoin him for dinner before their Leadville visit was through, and Kenton managed politely to evade a full acceptance.

They gave their good-byes. Mrs. Deverell reappeared, and Kenton kissed her narrow hand, pleasing her. The Deverells followed the journalists onto their porch and stood beaming after them until they were half a block away.

Kenton allowed himself a shudder. "Alex, I had to get out of there. That man has more hatreds than teeth."

"I noticed. At least his wife was nice."

"Too wrinkled. Never trust an overly wrinkled woman, Alex. I never met one yet who wouldn't put a knife in your back first chance."

"Sounds like Deverell's not the only one carrying around irrational prejudices."

Kenton protested, launching into a defense of his declaration. As he talked, Currell and Straker came riding out of an alley that led back to a well-hidden stable, apparently Deverell's. Currell nodded another greeting at the journalists, still with that troubled expression. Straker, though, was smiling. He looked at the journalists with open interest and gave a salutatory touch to the brim of his hat as he passed.

# Chapter 8

Mark Straker lit a cigarette and slumped in his saddle as he exhaled a cloud of fragrant smoke toward the sky. The late-summer day was cool and delightful. The hooves of the horses together made a pleasant syncopated rhythm on the evergreen-lined trail.

Straker liked a good smoke as well as a good ride, and enjoying the two simultaneously put him in a most mellow frame of mind. Currell, on the other hand, was tense and distant, as both he and Chop-off Johnson had often been since Jimmy Rhoder had been lynched. Straker found it mildly amusing, particularly since it was he and not the other two who could claim more reason to worry. After all, it was he who had actually committed the murder. Currell and Chop-off had done nothing but help him cover it up.

"So why are we doing this, Straker?" Currell asked suddenly after five full minutes of silence.

"Doing what?"

"Riding! Where the devil are we going?"

"The best place of all: nowhere in particular. You need to learn to relax, Currell. Enjoy things."

Currell swore and declared, "If it's to help me

relax that you brought me out here, you're wasting your time, and mine. I'm going back."

As Currell began to turn his mount, Straker raised a hand. "Wait, Currell, wait. There's more to it than that. I wanted to get you out here so we could talk in private. I tried to find Chop-off, too, but I couldn't."

"Out smoking opium somewhere, or drunk," Currell said. "I know his haunts—I can find him."

"Good, because you'll probably want him to help you when you go pull Jimmy Rhoder's corpse out of that mine shaft."

"The hell you say!" Currell's small eyes were suddenly much larger. "Why would I do that?"

Straker smiled. He was a man who enjoyed making plans; even more, he enjoyed sharing them, putting them into motion. And the more covert and clever, the better. That was how he had worked his way into his current position as one of Leadville's criminal leaders—a status of which only his carefully selected associates knew. Like his uncle-by-marriage Squire Deverell, Straker was ambitious and enterprising. Unlike his uncle, he was well liked in Leadville, liked in the way people always like cheerful, devil-may-care young men who were generous when it came time to buy the drinks.

"I've got plans for that corpse, Currell. Jimmy Rhoder can do us more good dead than he did us bad when he was alive. All we've got to do is string him up again where he can be found, and all your fear and fretting can come to an end."

Currell, his long hair blowing against his collar in the mountain breeze, stared disbelievingly at Straker, obviously thinking the man had gone mad.

Straker laughed. "Don't look at me like that, Currell—there's sense in what I'm saying. Hear me out."

"I'm listening. Anything as loco as what you're saying I got to hear."

"Tell me: Wasn't that pair who called on Uncle Squire this morning Brady Kenton and his partner?"

"Yeah. I know because I helped get them settled into the rooms above your uncle's new store building."

"Right. Why do you think Kenton's in Leadville at this time in particular?"

Currell shrugged. "Never gave it any thought."

"Give it some now."

After a couple of moments, Currell replied, "Because of the Briggs Garrett rumors?"

"Exactly. And I'm not just guessing when I say that. I know that Kenton's been going around asking questions about the Garrett stories in private. Of course, very little in Leadville stays private for long when you've got as many ears on the street as I have."

"So what's Brady Kenton and Briggs Garrett got to do with pulling Rhoder out of that hole?"

"Don't you see, Currell? Fate has just dealt us the best hand we could ask for. It's the way Jimmy died that makes the difference."

Currell frowned and shook his head. "I don't see what you're trying to say."

"Just that Briggs Garrett became infamous back in the war for hanging people and setting fire to their bodies. And now, conveniently, people believe he's alive and in Leadville—"

Suddenly Currell understood. "And Jimmy Rhoder died by hanging . . . and his body was burnt when the billiard hall went up!"

"Exactly, my friend. So if his corpse turns up in a roadside thicket somewhere, what is everyone going to think? That they've finally gotten solid proof that Garrett is alive and up to his old hanging and burning tricks again, and that Rhoder died at his hands. The results for us are obvious. Any potential suspicion in Rhoder's death would be thrown away from us. You and Chop-off could put aside your worries about being caught. Not that there's any reasonable chance we would be caught in any case."

Currell looked intrigued. He mulled it all over a moment or two. "But if you believe there's no reasonable chance of us getting caught as it is, why not leave it as it lays?"

"Because there's more to it than just diverting away any possible suspicion in that murder. There's also the matter of steering other suspicions in another direction. Toward my dear uncle Squire in particular."

Currell's expression showed he again did not understand.

Straker asked a question to illuminate his point. "Currell, what do you think would happen to a man in Leadville—particularly a man who was already hated in his own right—if enough people became convinced he was really Briggs Garrett, living under an assumed identity?"

"Hah! He'd wind up shot down or strung up, one or the other." Currell's expression changed again as soon as he had said the words. "Have mercy, Straker, are you thinking what I believe you are?"

Straker smiled darkly. "I'll be a well-off man, once I inherit Uncle Squire's holdings and mines. And a well-off man can afford to be very generous to those who have helped him get where he's gotten. You hear what I'm saying to you, Currell?"

Currell looked farther out the trail, to where the trees parted and afforded a splendid view of the high mountain country. Slowly he nodded. "I hear you."

Straker said, "I want you to go back into town and find Chop-off. Head out to the mine, and when it's dark, get Rhoder's corpse out of there and bring it back close to the edge of town. Find a place to hang it, a hidden place, but one where it will eventually be found. People have got to believe it's been hanging there several days. Somebody will find it soon enough."

"All right . . . but how will you make them believe your uncle is really Garrett?"

"Leave that to me. And to Brady Kenton."

"He's going to help you do this?"

"Indeed he is, though he doesn't know it. Come on, let's ride back. It may take you some time to find Chop-off. And you do understand, don't you, how important it is that no one see you at that mine?"

"I understand. Don't you worry—we'll make sure nothing goes wrong."

"You do that, Currell. You do that."

They turned their horses and rode back toward Leadville.

Kenton and Gunnison had gone to work after leaving Deverell's, dividing to sketch the town from different angles. Gunnison was on Chestnut Street, having been assigned the exercise of duplicating Kenton's earlier drawing of that avenue. Kenton and Gunnison were an unusual journalistic team in that each wrote and drew, rather than devoting himself to only one craft. Kenton, immensely talented in both areas, was unwilling to exercise only one of his skills. He knew what a prize he had in a partner who also possessed twin talents, even though both were less refined than his.

Kenton, having finished his preliminary sketch of a corner on Harrison, walked back to Chestnut and spotted Gunnison. As he approached from behind, he noted that Gunnison's pad lay at his feet, apparently having been dropped, and that Gunnison was standing as if frozen, staring up toward the top of a three-story narrow house that stood wedged between two store buildings across the street.

Kenton realized that he had caught his partner in the midst of a moment of amazement sufficient to have made him drop his sketch pad. Softening his step, Kenton came to Gunnison and clapped his hand suddenly on his shoulder.

Gunnison jumped, and Kenton grinned. "What's wrong, Alex? You look as if you've spotted a phantom."

"I think maybe I have," Gunnison replied breathlessly. "Look there!"

"Where?"

"The upper window! Look!"

Kenton did look, and saw nothing but an empty window. "I don't understand."

Gunnison was crestfallen. "She's gone."

"Who, for heaven's sake?"

"Kenton, I swear to you, just a moment ago, there was a girl there, looking out."

"Is that surprising?"

"Don't you see? That's the very window you had Victoria looking out of in your sketch last night! It was like seeing Victoria herself looking out at . . ."

Gunnison trailed off. The mention of Victoria had brought a stab of pain to Kenton, and it had shown on his face. He was also surprised; he had not known until that moment that Gunnison, or anyone else for that matter, had noticed his habit of subtly including Victoria's image in his sketches.

Kenton forced a smile and playful tone. "What you saw was just some young Leadville filly wondering who that good-looking fellow with the sketch pad was . . . and she probably wondered who that dandified boy with him was, too." Kenton forced a laugh at his own joke, then changed the subject. "Let me take a look at your sketch."

Gunnison picked up his pad and handed it to Kenton who examined the unfinished sketch, praising its good points, pointing out its weaknesses, suggesting improvements that could ease the strain on the wood-cutters who would later have to duplicate in reverse the pictures finally selected for publication.

But Kenton's mind was far from what he was doing. The mention of Victoria had swept a wave of sadness over him, and though he didn't want to admit it, he also felt strangely edgy beneath the empty gaze of that upper window. He wanted to be elsewhere. He had come to Leadville looking for a phantom of sorts—but not the phantom of his departed wife.

"Let's go back to the apartment," he said. "I've got things to do—and the best bet for you would be to write that fiancée of yours a letter. I know for a fact it's been too long since you have."

"I can't deny that," Gunnison said.

The pair began walking back to their lodgings. Before they were out of sight and while Gunnison was looking elsewhere, Kenton flashed a quick glance back down the street toward the window at which Gunnison had been staring. When he did, he saw a flash of movement there, as if a curtain had been dropped from the hand of someone behind it, someone watching the street.

Kenton quickly turned and looked ahead as something that felt like a cold hand clasped the back of his neck.

# Chapter 9

Kenton worked behind his closed door, so caught up in what he was doing that he hardly blinked as he watched the scene taking shape on the page before him under his trained pencil. This was a scene he had once vowed never to draw; now he could not restrain himself from doing it. Too long it had intruded into his sleeping dreams and waking thoughts—more so than ever now that he had talked to Victor Starlin.

His pencil made a great sweeping arc, leaving a line that became the edge of a ravine. Another sweep on the other side of the page made the ravine's opposite side. Bending over his table, Kenton etched in bushes, gaunt trees, shadows—many shadows. Finishing that, he sharpened his pencil, then began drawing a great skeletal structure of crosses and fractured lines. As the white sheet darkened with ever more lines, the vague structure took its shape. It was an image of ruin, and at its base Kenton drew flames, tiny feeble flames almost about to be extinguished but gushing thick spirals of smoke that blended with the shadows and the blackened beams composing the ruined skeletal thing spanning the ravine.

Then he drew the ropes, and at their ends the

seven limp figures that hung there side by side. Below
them he drew soldiers. On the page they were clad in
makeshift uniforms the color of his pencil lead, but in
the memory giving rise to the drawing, they wore
ragged butternut. At the foreground he at last began to
draw a final figure that bore a drawn saber. This figure
he sketched much closer and in much more detail—
until he came to the face. His pencil reached for the
paper, to draw in the features on the blank face . . . but
nothing would come. What was clear in his memory
Kenton could reproduce; what was vague and formless
he could not. The figure of the man with the saber he
could recall in detail, but the face was as featureless in
his memory as that of the sketched figure before him.

In a burst of frustration, Kenton ripped the paper
from his drawing table so violently that the table
overturned with a clatter. Wadding the sketch into a
ball, he threw it against the wall.

Alex Gunnison heard the table fall and wondered
what had happened. Folding the long letter he had
just written to his financée, he sealed it in its envelope,
then rose and walked to the door of Kenton's room.
"Are you all right?" he called.

"Of course I'm all right," Kenton called back,
sounding preoccupied. "The blasted table just collapsed
on me."

"You probably didn't close the clasp firmly enough,"
Gunnison commented.

"I know how my own table works, Alex."

Outside the door, Gunnison lifted his brows in
reaction to Kenton's hostile tone. Something surely was
on the man's mind. "I'll be gone for a while," Gunnison
said. "I've got this letter to mail."

"Then by all means go and mail it, and let me get
some work done."

"Good afternoon to you, too, Kenton."

\*    \*    \*

The sky had clouded, locking down against the earth the stench of the garbage dumps outside town. Gunnison found two long, slow-moving lines at the post office, divided according to surname initials. By the time his turn at the window came, much of the afternoon had waned. He briskly walked back to the apartment and knew even as he entered that Kenton was gone; he could smell the emptiness of the place.

*He's done it to me again,* Gunnison thought.

Kenton's door stood open, and Gunnison walked in, hoping Kenton had left a note. There was no note, but wadded sketches lay all around the room, obviously having been tossed randomly, as Kenton was prone to do on those rare occasions when he had to struggle over his work. Wondering what had posed such a challenge this time, Gunnison picked up one of the most finished-looking sketches.

It showed a burned-out bridge, a spindly framework of charred timbers running from ridge to ridge, overheated rails sagging toward the ground. From the bridge swung seven blackened corpses. Smoke rose from them as it did from the bridge. Men in a mix of Confederate uniforms and rough civilian clothing stood around them, one in particular prominent in the foreground. He was tall and broad, his face not drawn in.

Clearly this was a depiction of Briggs Garrett's burning of the Tennessee bridge burners. Gunnison remembered what Lundy O'Donovan had said about Briggs Garrett's supposedly being alive and in Leadville . . . and then something suddenly clicked into place in his mind, and it all became clear, leaving him amazed that he had not understood earlier.

Juan Cortez, the shepherd, had told Gunnison that the concern over which victor Starlin summoned Kenton had something to do with a "garrote." Or so Gunnison

had interpreted the word. Now he saw that what Cortez
had really been saying was not merely a word, but a
name: *Garrett*. Alex was chagrined that he had not
made that connection the moment Lundy O'Donovan
mentioned Garrett's name to him.

So it was true: Kenton had really come to Leadville
to hunt the infamous Briggs Garrett—to chase a ghost,
a rumor.

It all seemed unlikely and strange ... yet in another way it made sense. This was just the kind of
situation to intrigue Kenton, and Gunnison had to
admit it would make an interesting, though hardly
believable, story for the *Illustrated American*. But why
was Kenton being so secretive about his purpose?

Gunnison tossed the sketch back where he had
found it, and his eye fell on a crumpled envelope.
Recognizing it as the Victor Starlin letter Kenton had so
carefully kept from him, he picked it up with a sense of
gratification. Here, surely, would be more answers.

Removing the letter from the envelope, Gunnison
unfolded it. His eye at once picked a name out of the
ragged script: *Mickey Scarborough*.

Scarborough ... he knew that name. Mickey Scarborough was a traveling singer and showman who played
dance halls, opera houses and such throughout the
West. It seemed to Gunnison that he recalled seeing
something, a headline recently saying that Scarborough
had died. Yes—now he remembered: Scarborough had
died after collapsing on stage during a performance ... a
performance in Leadville.

Just as Gunnison was about to read the letter, a
wave of guilt stopped him. This was private mail.
Though it probably held information he wanted to
know, he had no right to read it.

Fighting back temptation, Gunnison put the letter

back in its place, left the room, and closed the door. Sometimes it was frustrating to be a decent person.

Never had Gunnison put much stock in coincidence, but it did seem remarkable that when he stepped out onto the street again minutes later, Briggs Garrett on his mind, there stood Lundy O'Donovan.

"I came back like I promised," he said. "Are you ready to go now?"

"That depends. Where are you taking me?"

Lundy glanced around and drew closer. "To an old mine, That's where we'll find him."

"Who? Briggs Garrett?"

He made a face as if to say *not so loud*. "Not Garrett, just a man he killed."

# Chapter 10

Gunnison blinked. "You want to take me to see a dead body?"

"That's right."

That one threw him off-kilter. "If you know where a dead body is, you need to go to the law," he suggested.

"No. I don't much trust the law around here."

"Why?"

"Marshal Duggan used to watch out for us, but since his term was up, things haven't been the same. After my papa died, the lot jumpers come in on me and Mama and Old Papa. Run us right out of our own home because they wanted the lot. Almost shot Old Papa, and him laid up in a chair like he is. Now we ain't got nothing but a little shack over on Chicken Hill. The law didn't help us at all." He paused. "Well? You coming with me or not?

Gunnison's answer might have been a firm refusal had it not been for the sketch he had just seen. His journalistic curiosity, not to mention a certain sense of competition with his senior partner, moved him. If in fact Kenton had come to Leadville looking for Garrett, it would be satisfying to be the one who found the first solid evidence concerning him . . . especially at a time

Kenton had again made himself absent without explanation.

"All right. I'll come."

Lundy grinned and without another word began walking. Gunnison fell in beside him.

He led them on a roundabout route. "Trying to make sure nobody can tell where we're going," he explained, and Gunnison began to suspect this was a rumor-inspired game of childish imagination. Nevertheless, he decided to play along for now, just in case.

"So how did you manage to find this body?" he asked.

"I'm always poking around. That's what my mama says about me. Always poking around, snooping into everybody's business, looking where I ain't supposed to look. Sometimes you see things folks thought was hid."

The sky had gone slate gray. Clouds and stinking sulphurous smelter smoke spread in layers over the town. Leadville was making a lot of people wealthy, but the pristine mountains were paying a big price for it.

Lundy led Gunnison through a portion of town he had not passed through before; it consisted almost entirely of spit-and-paper houses with big slabs for doors and barrels for chimney tops. Scattered along a nearby street were a half-dozen saloons housed in ramshackle little structures that managed to look ancient despite Leadville's short history. Resting miners coated with dirt and dried sweat sat beneath rickety overhanging saloon-porch roofs, sipping beer from glass and crockery mugs, eyeing passersby from beneath the brims of hats that had all but grown to their heads. Shaggy-haired, callused, weathered to a permanent deep brown, these men reminded Gunnison of earth-grubbing dwarfs pulled from some European fairy tale, given the gift of human stature and set down here beyond the Mosquito Range.

He followed Lundy down a dusty road and past a small graveyard lined with row upon row of fresh earthen mounds. Tombstones, or in many cases tomb boards, sat at cocked angles at the heads of them. A few graves were surrounded by small white fences, but these did little to cheer the burial ground. What little sunlight pierced through the clouds was meager illumination among the trees around the graveyard. The place gave Gunnison a chill, particularly when he considered that not one occupant of this cemetery had come to Leadville expecting any fate but wealth and good times for the rest of a long and happy life.

Lundy paused at the graveyard for a moment. "My papa's grave is there," he said, pointing. "I come here sometimes to talk to him."

They went on. Lundy tripped along at a steady rate, occasionally looking around and over his shoulder as if to make sure they weren't being watched or followed. Maybe he was leading an overly gullible journalist on a wild-goose chase, but he obviously had a specific destination.

"How far?" Gunnison asked.

"Few more minutes," he replied. "But I'm warning you, he smells foul as Judas's sin and looks worse."

"Hist!" Lundy said suddenly, stopping. He cocked his ear and listened to the air. Finally he shook his head. "Thought I heard something. Guess I didn't."

The country became more desolate. Here and there, isolated mining shacks looked down from hillsides or the heads of gulches, perched unnaturally where no man would expect to find them. Many of the forests had been stripped for firewood or building materials. There were enough stumps here to host every politician east of the Mississippi.

Behind them nothing of Leadville was visible but a smelter chimney and a few rooftops. One big ore wagon was rolling along just within sight, two men on the seat. Gunnison could not tell if they had seen him and Lundy and did not mention them.

Shortly afterward, Lundy stopped. "There's where we'll find him."

He was pointing to a wooden structure built so naturally against the hillside that Gunnison had not even noticed it. At first Gunnison took it for a cabin, then saw that it sheltered a mine entrance. But there was no evidence of recent activity hereabouts; perhaps this mine had shown promise early on but gave out. Obviously it was abandoned now.

"Whose is this?" Gunnison asked.

"Squire Deverell grubstaked it. Never came to nothing."

A putrid smell reached Gunnison's nose. Not overpowering, not even all that noticeable . . . but it was the unmistakable smell of death. Suddenly the sky was more gray, the land more barren, the weathered mine entrance more foreboding.

"Well, we going in?" Lundy asked. His dirty little face looked strangely impish.

"Lundy, you swear this isn't a joke?"

"Swear on my papa's grave."

Lundy handed him a box of matches and a candle stub, and they walked toward the door.

*Sure wish Kenton were here,* Gunnison thought. *Bet this wouldn't make him nervous a bit. Bet he'd march right in, find out it's just a dead mongrel, and have a good laugh at his own expense.* Swallowing, he pulled at the door. It popped off its only remaining hinge and fell to the side. Man and boy stepped inside.

The smell of death was much stronger. They lit their candles.

"Where is the shaft?" Gunnison asked.

"Yonder. He's at the bottom."

"How deep?"

"Not very. They gave up on this hole early on. I'd say he's maybe twenty-five feet down."

Holding up his candle, Gunnison made out the shaft opening a few yards back into the hillside against which the entrance shelter was built. A wooden railing had been built for safety around the hole, and into the hole extended a worn rope hanging from a winch above and tucked under a closed trapdoor atop the shaft. Gunnison opened the trapdoor and moved the rope; it swung freely, the ore bucket obviously having been removed for use elsewhere.

The death stench was indeed rising from the shaft and had grown stronger the moment he lifted the trapdoor. The flame of the candle he held began to dance a bit as a fit of trembling came over him. It wouldn't have taken much to make him leave, but an image of Kenton's scowling face came to mind. Kenton wouldn't turn away from something like this, so neither would he. Resolutely, he pulled a handkerchief from his pocket and tied it across his nose and mouth in an attempt to cut the stench. "How do we get down?" Gunnison asked through the masking cloth.

Lundy lowered his candle, and by its light Gunnison saw that rungs had been built down one side of the shaft.

Suddenly Lundy looked alarmed. "Listen!" he whispered.

Gunnison heard nothing but the wind. "What did you hear?"

Lundy shook his head as before. "Nothing, I guess.

I'm just nervous. This could be dangerous if we were to be caught by the wrong people, you know."

He was right, and that didn't make Gunnison feel any better. The ore wagon he had seen came to mind, and he almost mentioned it but then did not, reminding himself that this probably was merely Lundy's fantasy and whatever was making the smell was likely as not a dead dog—though a big one, judging from the stench it generated.

He steeled his nerve. "Well, I'm going down." The first rung creaked under his weight; his candle flame flickered and threatened to go out "Wish we had lanterns," he said. He went down several more rungs until Lundy's face was small and far above, framed in the dim square of the shaft's top frame.

The smell was becoming stifling. He wrinkled his nose and tried to shut out the stench as he descended clumsily, having to hold on to the candle and the rungs as well. The dangling rope brushed him as he went down.

Something moved beside him. He thought at first it was a a rat perched on an unseen ledge or peering out of a hole. In fact it was simply a piece of cloth hung on a big nail sticking out from the shaft framing. One edge of it was burned.

Lundy saw that Gunnison had stopped. "What did you find?"

"Piece of a shirt or something. Burnt."

"Must have tore off the body when they dropped it down."

"Why would it be burnt?"

"Because Briggs Garrett burns those he kills. Ain't you heard the stories?"

Gunnison stopped, not sure now he would continue. The smell was so terrible, he wasn't sure he could breathe at the bottom in any case. His stomach was beginning to lurch. "You're telling me the corpse is burnt?" he asked a little shakily.

Lundy didn't answer; in fact, Lundy suddenly was gone. A moment later came his scream, then the sound of scuffling, a man's voice, another scream from Lundy. The trapdoor atop the shaft closed, shutting out all the meager light from above and creating a sudden downdraft of air that blew Gunnison's candle dead.

Gunnison was in pitch blackness, a thick death stench rising from below, some sort of violence going on above. Panic threatened to rise within, but he stifled it. Forcing himself to become calm, he dug matches from his pocket and relit the candle stub. Then he began to climb.

More scuffling above, then silence.

"Lundy!" Gunnison yelled.

No answer. He was nearer the trapdoor now.

"Lundy?" His call was softer this time. He had reached the top of the shaft. Pausing for a moment, he gathered his resolve and pushed the trapdoor open.

The toe of a boot caught him on the side of the head, jarring him loose from the ladder and sending him down. The trapdoor closed again, he fell for what seemed half an eternity squeezed into a quarter of a second, then by pure luck his hands caught the knotted end of the rope, slowing his fall at the last possible instant. But he continued to fall, and the thing he struck at bottom was stiff and reeking, all the more horrible for being unseen. He heard a yell go echoing up the shaft and realized it was his own.

Stunned but not unconscious, Gunnison scrambled up off the foul thing that he would later realize had probably saved him from death or severe injury against the hard rock and dirt below it. He dug again in his pocket for his matches, lit one—and let out another shout when he saw what lay on the floor at his feet.

Gunnison had expected ugliness, but this burned eyeless corpse, a cut rope tailing from its rat-chewed neck, was foul beyond description. Panicked, he turned and bolted out of pure instinct into the darkness, promptly pounded his head hard against the base of the shaft ladder, and collapsed to the floor, senseless.

# Chapter 11

Brady Kenton scratched a day's worth of whiskers and looked up to study the gaudy sign swinging above a nearby saloon. Or so he appeared to be doing, for in fact he was taking a backward glance. His suspicion was confirmed—they were still following him. Had been since he had left a saloon farther up the street where he had conducted another series of unproductive inquiries aimed at finding what truth might lie behind the Garrett rumors.

Casually he began to whistle, and slipped his right hand into his pocket. In the process he brought it close to the grip of his pistol. The street was teeming, as usual, and Kenton hoped he could lose himself in the crowd.

His trained eye had already sized up his two followers. Both were in their twenties, the first a lean man who wore ragged town clothing. He looked like a dry-goods clerk gone to seed. His hair was combed straight back and slick with either a hair tonic or its own oil. The other, dressed in the ragged style of a cowboy, was taller and big around the gut. Both wore their jackets in a way that indicated they had weapons hidden from the watchful Leadville police force.

Kenton suspected that he knew why he was being followed. His inquiries about Garrett had been subtle and covert. He had not even revealed his purposes to his own partner and had deliberately deserted him twice now to allow for private investigation. But obviously the fact had reached the streets that he was in town looking into the Garrett rumors. Given Garrett's infamy, it was no surprise that two gunmen like these would be interested in anyone who they believed could lead them to a prize so legendary. Kenton wished, for the first time ever, that the *Illustrated American* had not chosen to run a portrait of him in every edition. He was too easily recognized now by such as the two behind him. The irony was, he couldn't guide them to Garrett if he wanted to. So far, his investigation had revealed nothing substantial; he did not even know if Garrett was alive.

They were closer now. That was not good. Kenton had hoped that their intention had been simply to follow him on the possibility that he would guide them to Garrett. Now he doubted that. Probably they hoped to get him into some hidden place and threaten or beat the information out of him. The thought made his blood hot. He was growing weary of these two.

Quickly he made a right turn, then trotted down half a block and right into an alley. At the end of it stood a woodshed, with the door ajar. In a handful of seconds Kenton was inside.

He saw them pass at the far end of the alley—silhouettes against the background of a well-lit dance hall among the buildings on the other side of the street. Kenton paused a few moments, then emerged, smiling with satisfaction. They were gone.

Just as he started back up the alley toward the street, he saw them again. They had obviously detected that he had evaded them and returned to the alley as the most likely spot into which he could have ducked. Too late now to do anything; though it was dark, he knew he was seen.

"Hello, Brady Kenton," said the bigger man, advancing one step and quietly drawing his pistol. "You'll be so kind as to stand still right there, now, won't you?"

Kenton drew his own pistol, cocked it, and leveled it at the man, who immediately stopped advancing. By now, the smaller of the pair had also drawn a pistol.

"Looks like we've got a standoff," Kenton commented.

"Looks like it—and there's no reason for it, either. All we want is information, not trouble."

"Any information I've got generally goes into the pages of the *Illustrated American*," Kenton replied. "I don't hand it out for free on the street."

"Let's drop the games and lay it out straight, Kenton. Where's Briggs Garrett?"

"Around every corner, based on what I'm hearing."

The big man's face was hidden in shadows, but a tightening of the atmosphere let Kenton know that the fellow was becoming more tense. "Don't waste my time, Kenton. Talk or I'll drop you."

"Be careful, friend. I might take that as a threat and decide I'm justified in dropping you first."

The smaller man stepped forward. "Try talking that way to me," he said.

"Shut up," said the other. "He ain't told us yet." No sooner had he said it than a solid *thunk* resounded and he collapsed to his knees.

"Down you go, Smithfield," a voice from behind the gunmen cheerfully declared.

The other gunman wheeled, and the pistol butt that had just crashed into the crown of his big partner's head smashed into his forehead. He slammed back under the impact and gave himself a follow-up blow to the back of the head when he pounded into the brick wall. There the fellow leaned for several moments, arms outstretched, his pistol still held. A dark form stepped closer to him, and there was yet another *thunk*. Now the man collapsed.

"And so much for you, Raglow," the new arrival said.

Kenton, as surprised as he was gratified by the unexpected aid, lowered his pistol but did not yet holster it. He aired a suspicion. "Percival Starlin?"

"Perk, dang it, Perk! Percival's a flower-plucking name."

Kenton grinned, holstered his pistol, and stepped forward, putting out his hand. "Pleased to meet you, Perk. Victor told me you were a helpful man. I see now he was right."

"Ah, it's nothing. I seen these two on your tail and figured it might be a good time to make your aquaintance. Victor wrote me that you was coming, you know."

"Perk Starlin, I'd like to buy you a beer, if you're willing."

"Well, normally I don't drink . . . but for you I'll make an exception. Come on—I'll take you to my favorite place for not drinking."

Perk Starlin took Kenton to the crudest of taverns—haphazardly built, unpainted inside and out, its lumber walls almost as rough and gnarly as the human patrons they protected from the Colorado night.

The place brought back memories to Kenton of a thousand similar nameless dives he had known in his time, sometimes as a journalist trying to capture the gritty kind of reality that could not be found elsewhere, sometimes as a private man trying to forget that same reality and the pain it had brought him. The latter never really worked; Kenton had discovered that no problem got any better for being baptized in whiskey.

From the corner came the music of a Mexican guitarist, who was managing quite well despite the absence of two strings. Bottles clinked, glassed clumped tabletops, wooden poker chips rattled. Perk Starlin sat across from him, drinking a beer with the relish of a connoisseur. Kenton detected a vague family similarity between Perk and Victor Starlin, though in build the two were radically different. Whereas Victor was lean and spindly, Perk was very stout and several inches shorter than his sheepherding cousin. His chest was like a barrel, his arms and legs like sections of stovepipe— but it was muscle, not fat, that gave the man his stoutness.

"Their names are Raglow and Smithfield—can't say I really know them. Just know *of* them is all. They're two leftover gunnies from the railroad war, and both are pokes of trouble looking for a place to bust. Just the sort to see Briggs Garrett as a prize fish."

"Well, if they think I can put Garrett on their hook, they're dead wrong."

"Cold trail?"

"Not cold, just not really warm either. I've been asking questions on the sneak since I got here, and all I've picked up are rumors, most of them contradicting each other. The only common theme I can find is that half of Leadville seems to believe that Briggs Garrett is alive and somewhere in this city."

"And why do you care whether he is or not?" Perk asked with an expression that indicated he might already know the answer.

"Has Victor told you much about that?" Kenton asked in return.

Perk gave a slight smile. "He's told me enough.

You and Victor have a personal interest in Garrett . . . just like Mickey Scarborough did."

"That we do. Tell me about Scarborough, Perk. Tell me what happened."

"What happened was that the man collapsed, raving right there on the stage, and what he hollered out is the thing that started all these rumors about Garrett."

"They tell me he saw Garrett right there in the audience."

"So he did, or at least, so he declared. 'Garrett!' he yelled. 'Briggs Garrett!' Threw out a finger to point, but he collapsed right there, and nobody could see who he was trying to show. Fell in a heap, he did, and died in Ella Chrisman's house. I helped carry him there."

"Who's this Ella Chrisman?"

"Some sort of nurse or some such. A lot of talk here about that woman. She's divorced, you see—and rich from what her husband left her when they gave each other the heave."

"Why didn't they take Scarborough to the St. Vincent Hospital instead of Mrs. Chrisman's?"

"She was in the crowd and asked special that he be brought there, for one thing. And her house was close by. I suppose that was it."

"Has Mrs. Chrisman ever taken in other ill people like she did Mickey Scarborough?"

"Not that I know of. Anyway, once he died, the whole dang town was full of talk. Briggs Garrett, alive and in Leadville! The story spread far enough that even Victor heard about it, down on Austin Bluffs."

Kenton nodded. "He heard it, all right, and it knocked him back enough that he sent me a letter asking me to come to him. Told me that if Garrett is really alive, I would be the man most able to find him."

# Chapter 12

Perk sat his chair upright and leaned in closer to Kenton. "But Garrett can't be alive, can he? He was drowned long ago. All the papers had a story about it. Even the *Illustrated American*. I read it myself."

"So did I. Look, Perk, I can't make any more sense of this than anyone else. I can't believe that Garrett is really alive...but then, I can't believe that Mickey Scarborough would be mistaken if he claimed to see him. If there's a man who would know Briggs Garrett's face, it was Mickey. And Garrett's body never was recovered, so there's no grave to dig up and check."

A broadly constructed saloon girl who smelled of too much saloon and too little soap walked by and smiled down at Perk. Perk smiled back and watched her with much more appreciation than Kenton thought she merited as she waddled back to the bar. Only when she went behind it did Perk shift his attention back to Kenton. "So how can I help you out?"

"You've already helped me plenty by busting those heads outside."

"Aw, that was nothing. If they had fought, it might have been more fun. I've always enjoyed a good row.

73

Come on, now—tell me what I can do. I'd like to help you find Garrett."

"Then the thing to do is keep your ears and eyes open, and ask a few questions when you can do it without drawing attention. Let me know what's being said on the streets. You can find me above Squire Deverell's new store, the one on Harrison that's not open yet. I've got a partner named Alex Gunnison, a young fellow. Where can I find you, Perk?"

"I'm a watchman from time to time over at the James Stables, north end of Spruce. Other than that I'm either just out and about town or at my cabin down the road toward Malta." He gave brief instructions that Kenton mentally filed.

The two men talked longer and drank one more beer each. The guitarist broke another string and quit. Kenton and Perk parted ways then, Perk heading for his job at the stables.

Kenton had it in mind to head back to his rooms where he expected an angry Gunnison awaiting him. He dreaded the encounter. Kenton didn't like running out and leaving his partner alone, but this search still seemed too vague—and too personal—to involve Gunnison. Soon, though, he would tell him what was going on—just as soon as he had something substantial enough to tell.

Something jostled Alex Gunnison roughly, and a gruff voice growled out garbled words in an Irish brogue. He felt himself being rolled over, and the words this time became clear: "Give me your money—give me your money, damn your eyes..."

Gunnison opened his eyes, strained them into focus. The jostling continued. "Leave me... alone," he managed to say after he managed to dig his voice out of the clogged well of his throat.

"Leave you alone I will, once you give me your money!" the man said. Gunnison groaned and looked at his troubler who was crouched beside him in a decidedly insectlike posture. He wore the tattered remnants of a seafarer's outfit. A potent smell of whiskey hung about him like a heavy cloak. His reddish face, masked in a rind of dirt, glowered down at Gunnison.

"Leave me alone!" This time Gunnison was able to speak with more force and at the same time swing up his arm. Almost randomly the side of his hand struck the man on the side of the face.

He swore loudly and pulled back, then wobbled and fell on his back. Gunnison rolled over, away from him, and tried to get up. The drunken seaman stood, wobbled some more, then tried to kick Gunnison. The kick went ridiculously wild, its force on the upswing pulling the man's other leg out from beneath him. He fell with a loud grunt on his back, groaned, then passed out.

Gunnison finally managed to stand and staggered over to a hitchpost. Something was wrong here, unexplainable, impossible, but he could not clear his clouded mind enough to comprehend what it was. Looking blearily around, trying to keep on his feet, he wondered where he was and how he had come to be here. He was supposed to be somewhere else ... somewhere else ... but where?

He staggered away, fearing the drunken man would rise again, and rounded a corner where he stopped and leaned, breathless, against a wall. Every muscle ached, and he was sure his entire left side was extensively bruised. He noticed that he had not left behind the strong smell of whiskey with the fallen man; it hung about his own clothing as strongly as if he had been soaked in it. Feeling his shirt, he found it damp. He *had* been soaked in whiskey.

Nothing made sense. Surely it was a dream. He recognized now where he was: Stillborn Alley, a well-known Leadville alleyway where many a corpse had been found, including some of the stillborn offspring of diseased prostitutes. So he was in town, back from ... where? He had left Leadville, that he recalled, and gone somewhere, seen something, fallen into a deep hole ...

The whiskey smell was about to make Gunnison sick. Like everything else in this situation, it seemed distorted and abnormal. Examining himself in the dim light that reflected from some gambling parlor, he saw that his clothing was incredibly foul. He was mud-streaked, tattered, and badly spotted with some unidentifiable substance that was not dirt, not blood, nor anything he could identify. The substance was exuding a putrid stench that mixed with and altered the smell of the whiskey on him. A more revolting stench he could not have had attached to him, short of having a burned cat cadaver hung about his neck.

Burned ...

There was something significant in that, something that teased his mind.

Images were beginning to come back. Not full memories, just fragments. Very unpleasant fragments.

A black hole, his body falling into it ... a young boy yelling in fear ... a stench boring into his nostrils, making him sick ... the feeling of having descended into a hell pit and meeting the devil at the bottom ...

"But how did I get back to town?" he asked aloud. There was no one there to answer. *Got to get back home*, he thought—*if I can remember where home is. Kenton—got to find Kenton.*

Gunnison knew he was in bad shape. Something he had experienced had hurt him physically and also severely disoriented him mentally. He needed rest, a good wash, and maybe medical help.

But mostly he needed to know what it was that was hammering at the back of his consciousness, wanting to get in. Something was wrong somewhere, badly wrong. Someone was in danger, but when Gunnison tried to remember who, and how, and why, it amounted to mining a dry hole. *Have to find Kenton*, he thought. *Have to get home, and if my memory can't guide me, maybe my instincts will.*

With that, he took a deep breath that hurt the left side of his rib cage badly, then set off into a street that teemed with a nation's worth of people and seemed to run ten miles in both directions. Groaning aloud, he chose right over left and began limping down the boardwalk, drawing stares all along the way.

# Chapter 13

When he first saw the policeman dragging along the drunk, Kenton found it humorous.

The officer, a staunch-looking fellow in the standard Leadville blue uniform, was towing a young drunk roughly up the street, one hand gripping his elbow, the other twisting his ear to discourage any thought of running away. Strangely, the officer was holding the drunk as far away from him as he could and had his head turned away. On his face was the offended expression of a man carrying a sack of rotting fish.

Kenton grinned, but his grin faded abruptly when something drew his attention away from the policeman to the drunk. Brady Kenton had lived too long to be surprised by much, but he was surprised now.

The drunk was none other than Alex Gunnison.

The journalist made sure his pistol was well hidden beneath his jacket and walked toward the officer, eyeing Gunnison all the way. The young man looked terrible; he was covered with muck, and his hair was so sodden and disheveled that he looked like a man just yanked out of a long-term sickbed.

Gunnison's bleary eyes fell on Kenton when he was about twenty feet away. "Kenton!" he said, sounding a little more vigorous than his looks would lead one to anticipate. "Thank God!"

The smell of whiskey reached Kenton's nostrils; Gunnison reeked as if he had bathed in a whiskey barrel. But the smell of liquor was mixed with a putrid dead stench.

"Here now—who are you?" the officer asked Kenton suspiciously.

"I'm Brady Kenton," he replied. "And this, uh, drunk . . . he's my partner."

"Brady Kenton? Of the *Illustrated American?*"

"Yes."

"Aye, I heard you were in town." He gave Gunnison a shake. "I must say, Mr. Brady Kenton, that you could stand keeping a tighter leash on your companion."

"So I can see. Alex, what's happened to you?"

"I don't remember . . . there was a hole, something foul and dead, and trouble—trouble I can't remember. I don't know how I got here, Kenton. I was somewhere else, I can't remember where, and then I woke up and I was lying in an alley."

Kenton's surprise was turning to concern. Gunnison seemed distraught and disoriented, maybe injured. There was more to this than simple drunkenness . . . and Gunnison rarely drank at all.

"Officer, may I ask you a favor? I'd like to ask that you show some mercy in this particular case and turn my partner over into my custody."

"Mercy? By the saints, I wish this lad would have considered showing mercy to poor old Clance Sullivan and not go wandering the streets in such a state. I found him staggering about, scaring the wits out of every decent soul he passed—and for that I can scarce blame them, smelling like he does." The policeman had the strong accent of an Irish commoner.

"Please, officer. I'll see him to his bed and keep him there until he's fit to get out."

The policeman seemed interested. On any particular night in Leadville there were plenty of other concerns besides one staggering young sot to keep him busy. "Aye . . . well, Mr. Kenton, I'm told you are a man of good standing, and I'm inclined to take you up on your kind offer. Lord knows I'm not eager to have this one stinking up the jail the rest of the night."

"I'll see he gets a good washing-down in the bargain," Kenton said.

The officer let go of Gunnison's arm and steered him by the ear over to Kenton. "Take him and be gone, then."

"Thank you, Officer Sullivan. You are a decent man."

"Just a tired old street plodder is what I am, and if ever you want to have a sad story for your *Illustrated American,* just come and let poor old Clance Sullivan tell you about his woes."

"I may do that, sir, if you are serious. Thank you again."

"Off with you both. Go on."

Gunnison leaned over the washbasin and scrubbed the filth from his hair. His clothing lay in a reeking heap in the corner, and the floor was damp from his splashing in the basin. It was ten minutes past midnight.

The cleansing of his body was bringing refreshment and new strength to Gunnison, but his feeling of distress and a forgotten danger that cried out for remembering was only growing stronger. Kenton stood near his side, looking worried, questioning Gunnison closely.

Gunnison hardly heard the questions, for the images that had flashed across his mind since his awakening were more frequent now, and more detailed, occupying his full attention. Memory was beginning to stir: A pit, darkness... a mine shaft. Climbing down a ladder... a burned rag of cloth on a nail... the death smell from below...

"If I had to guess the smell of what was on you, Alex," Kenton was saying, "I would say it was burnt flesh. Not only burnt, but decaying. Mighty strange thing."

Burned flesh... a body, at the bottom of the pit... a rope around the neck... a voice crying out above, a child's voice...

*Lundy O'Donovan.*

Gunnison shuddered and leaned forward weakly against the washstand as full memory flooded back. The basin tilted and fell with a clatter to the floor, sending water flying.

"Alex!"

"Kenton, I remember now, I remember." Gunnison turned to Kenton, grasped his shoulders. "Lundy O'Donovan is in danger, Kenton. We've got to find him before it's too late—if it's not too late already."

"In danger? Lundy O'Donovan? Are you addled, Alex?"

"In the name of heaven, Kenton, don't doubt me now! You have to listen: Lundy O'Donovan may have been taken... may have been killed!"

"Killed? By whom?"

Gunnison took a deep breath and forced himself to become calm. He ran his fingers through his wet hair. "I don't know. But maybe by Briggs Garrett."

Kenton's expression became as black as a thundercloud. He drew in a sharp breath and stiffened, his eyes growing fiery.

"I remember it all now, Kenton. There's a place we

must go at once. An abandoned mine, with a dead man inside. I'll explain along the way—and if we can, we need to take a police officer with us."

"Are you well enough to lead us there, Alex?"

"Yes, yes! But we have to hurry—Lundy's life may depend on it."

Kenton nodded. "Get on some fresh clothes, then. I'll see to the pistols.

# Chapter 14

Even before they reached the street, Gunnison had given Kenton a brief but sufficient explanation of his excursion with Lundy and the mystifying experiences at the mine and thereafter. Most mystifying of all was how Gunnison had traveled from the bottom of the mine all the way to Stillborn Alley and how he had come to be doused in liquor. Kenton had no more explanation for that than Gunnison.

The conventional wisdom that policeman are easy to find when you don't need one and impossible to find when you do proved to be as true in Leadville as it was anywhere else. On the street were enough drunks, soiled doves, and footpads to fill Hades's quota, but a policeman was not to be seen.

"We'll have to go on alone," Kenton said. "It's likely we'd have a devil of a time convincing a policeman to believe us at any rate."

"Believe what, may I ask?" The voice was Clance Sullivan's, spoken from a dark store-porch corner nearby. He stepped into the triangle of light cast by a window, looked at Gunnison. "You appear to have sobered peculiarly fast, my young friend."

83

"I wasn't drunk in the first place," Gunnison returned.

"Sullivan, you're a godsend," Kenton said. "You've got to come with us. We've got a missing little boy by the name of Lundy O'Donovan on our hands, and he may be in danger."

"Lundy? Aye, I know the lad. He lives on Chicken Hill with his mother and that poor old grandfather of his."

"Maybe we should look there first," Gunnison suggested. "He might be at home."

"I think not," the policeman said. "I saw his mother come up this very street not ten minutes ago, calling for him. He wanders a lot, that lad, and I've seen her out looking for him often. And that's a bad thing, for she has to leave the old grandfather alone to do it, and alone he doesn't need to be."

"Lundy may still be at the mine, then," Gunnison said. "We'd best hurry."

"Mine?" Sullivan asked. "What mine?"

"Officer Sullivan," Kenton said hurriedly, "I want you to listen to what Alex here has to say. It's a strange story, one you may not be prone to believe, but I can vouch for his character. If he says a thing is true, then it is."

Sullivan sighed, obviously sensing that the rest of his night's duty was to be busy.

"All right," he said to Gunnison. "Tell me your story."

Lantern light made the interior of the mine entrance shed eerie, casting inky shadows that crept around the walls as the lanterns moved. The lanterns had been in the back of a miner's wagon Clance Sullivan had commandeered in the name of the Leadville Department of Police. Its owner had made the mistake of driving into town as Kenton's party was going out of it, and despite the man's protests, Sullivan had taken his rig, giving promises of its safe return and maybe even compensation, though warning the fellow shouldn't count on the latter. Sullivan had then driven the wagon as if he were trying to break the axles. Gunnison did not know if he had believed his story or simply felt compelled to treat it as potentially true.

Into the shaft they descended, Kenton first, Sullivan second, Gunnison last. The lanterns cast much more light in the hole than had Gunnison's feeble candle on his descent, but that only heightened his sense of being swallowed by the earth itself. A lingering scent of death hung in the air but seemed much lessened for some reason.

When they reached the bottom, Gunnison understood why: The body was gone. "I don't understand," he said. "It was right here—I fell on it, got up, got my candle lit again, and there it was. I swear it!"

Two silent, dirty faces looked at him.

"I swear it!" he repeated. Kneeling, he said, "There at least has to be ash left from where it lay." But the lantern light revealed none. The ground was clean.

"They must have swept it, or put fresh dirt on top of it," Gunnison said feebly, knowing how unbelievable his story was beginning to sound.

"There *is* a rotting smell remaining," Kenton said, seeking to lessen his partner's incredibility. "That at least shows something dead has been hereabouts."

"Many a dead critter can be found in these old holes," Sullivan said. He was looking at Gunnison with disgust. "They crawl back into crevices and such, and die." Then to Gunnison: "By the saints, young fellow, you've led this old Irishman on a fool's errand!"

"Somebody's taken the body," Gunnison protested. "I vow to you, it was right here."

"I think perhaps you're not as sober as you look," Sullivan said. "I should have taken you to a cell and saved myself all this trouble. And me all but stealing a wagon for the sake of it! I may catch some trouble over that, you know."

There was nothing to say. Gunnison turned to Kenton, hoping to find evidence he believed him, but he couldn't tell if he did or not.

"Perhaps we'd best leave now," Kenton said quietly.

"The body had a rope around its neck," Gunnison said. "he'd been hanged and burned—just like those bridge burners Briggs Garrett killed, Kenton."

At the mention of Garrett, Sullivan looked at Gunnison intently. "What name did you call?"

"Briggs Garrett."

"Why? You know aught of him?"

"We've heard stories, rumors" Kenton said. "Have you?"

"Aye. But it's foolish and idle talk, dangerous to be spread. You forget all about Briggs Garrett and burnt dead men in mine shafts." He barked it out with fervor. Suddenly he stopped, as if realizing something. His anger rose as if a bellows had been put to it. "Ah, now I see it! The famed Brady Kenton and his partner come to Leadville and stir the latest gossip a bit, then make up tales to make the local law look foolish for the sake of a good story! That's your game, is it? I should jail the both of you!"

"You're wrong," Kenton said calmly. "We don't work that way." He paused, then committed himself. "If Alex says there was a body here, then there was a body here."

"Is that right? You know what Clance Sullivan says? I say you're either liars or drunkards or both! And I also say you'll not ride by my side back to Leadville! Walk until you're more honest men, the both of you!" He turned and began climbing up the rungs, taking one of the lanterns with him. Part of the way up, he stiffened and grunted, almost dropping the lantern.

"Sullivan?" Kenton said in concern.

"Leave it be, leave it be," he responded angrily. "My arm again—hurts from time to time—particularly so after giving aid to fools." After that last jab, he resumed climbing until he was up and out.

Kenton and Gunnison looked at each other. "You really do believe me?" Gunnison asked.

"I do," Kenton said. "I might be inclined to blame it all on that blow to your noggin, but I saw the filth on you. I smelled it, and I know the smell of burnt flesh." He paused. "Know it far too well."

"But where's the body now?"

"Even more important—where's Lundy O'Donovan?"

Lundy—Gunnison had all but forgotten him. "We'd best begin looking, and fast," he said.

They climbed up the ladder. Sullivan was above, no less angry for the passage of a few moments. "I'll take that lantern, too," he said.

"We need at least one lantern to look for the missing boy," Kenton replied.

"There's no missing boy any more than there is a missing body," Sullivan replied. "I'll not be held guilty for the theft of a lantern—give it to me." He stalked off to the wagon with a lantern in each hand, extinguished them, and drove off.

Kenton and Gunnison were left in the dark. They called for Lundy and tried to search, but the night was too black to see, and no one answered. Kenton at last declared they should return to Leadville and try to find Lundy's house; perhaps the boy had returned on his own during the last hour.

The walk back to Leadville was difficult because of their weariness, the darkness, and in Gunnison's case, extensive soreness and bruises. Still, he was pleased to be able to move about at all. His fall, which could have been fatal, had done him no significant injury, thanks to the cushioning corpse at the bottom of the shaft.

"The most loco thing about all this, when you think about it," said Kenton, "is why whatever scoundrel who did all this took such pains to spare your life. To haul you out of the shaft, take you back to town, soak you in whiskey—that's a lot more troublesome than simply bashing in your skull and leaving you to rot."

"That's a pleasant thought," Gunnison said ironically. But Kenton had raised a good point. "If he was that merciful to me, maybe he was to Lundy, too."

"So we may hope. But the question remains why someone who would hang and burn one man would have a streak of mercy at all. It's not very logical. Especially if it really is Garrett. Garrett never knew the meaning of mercy." He touched the scar on his cheek.

Gunnison paused, then asked, "Kenton, am I right that you brought us to Leadville to find Briggs Garrett?"

Kenton did not answer for a couple of moments. "Yes," he said finally in a low voice.

"For the sake of getting the story?"

"For much more than that," Kenton replied.

Gunnison had developed an instinctive feeling for when Kenton could be safely pressed and when he could not. This was one of the latter times. They fell silent, concentrating on their walking. Leadville lay ahead, twinkling in the blackness.

# Chapter 15

By the time Mark Straker finished cursing, he was out of both expletives and breath. George Currell stood before him with an expression that combined worry and anger, watching Straker pace back and forth. The night sky spread above, and the wind whipped through the surrounding trees. It was here, at Currell's hut near Poverty Flat, that Straker awaited the return of his accomplices from the mine where Jimmy Rhoder's body had been hidden. They should have returned with news of a mission accomplished. Instead they had brought a most distressing story.

Straker could not believe such a simple job as removing a corpse from an abandoned mine shaft could have taken such a devastating turn. Currell had told him in a shaking voice that when they arrived at the mine, two people were already there. One was the little O'Donovan boy from Chicken Hill, a fatherless ragamuffin whom most of Leadville's longer-term residents knew from his nearly continuous presence on the streets. The other was Alex Gunnison, partner of Brady Kenton.

That was as far as the story had gotten before

Straker began cursing and pacing. Now he stopped, took a deep breath, and faced Currell again.

"They saw you, I suppose."

"The boy did. Gunnison didn't. He was in the shaft when we came in, and I kicked him in the head when he stuck it up out of the hole. He fell back in on top of Rhoder and got knocked out cold. Never saw a thing."

"So what did you do with the boy?"

"Chop-off grabbed him, and he let out a yell and pulled loose. I went for him, but he got out the door. I couldn't catch him."

"So he saw your faces, and now he's out running loose?" Straker swore some more as he lifted his hands skyward in exasperation. "You know what this means, don't you? This means that once he talks, it won't be Briggs Garrett people associate with that corpse, but you and Chop-off! But wait—where's this Gunnison now?"

Currell swallowed nervously. "Chop-off wanted to kill him. I said no—I'm not going to get involved in another murder. So we drug him out of the hole. Chop-off had about half a bottle of whiskey with him, and we soaked Gunnison with it, hauled him back to town, and dumped him in Stillborn Alley. We were careful—nobody saw us."

"But why in the name of—"

"Don't you see, Straker? Ain't nobody going to believe anything he says now. They'll say he was drunk and dreamed it all up."

Straker thought about it and grudgingly had to admire Currell's cleverness. The admiration faded with a new realization, however. "But Rhoder's body— somebody is bound to check the mine and find it."

"Rhoder's not in the mine anymore," Currell said. "We knew we couldn't leave him, but we couldn't string him up somewhere like you said to do, either, not with that kid likely to squall out that he had seen us at the mine. We threw Rhoder's body into a little cave-hole on past the mine. We heard it splash into water a long way down. He won't be found by nobody now."

"That's good at least. Ruins my plan about uncle Squire though. And there's still the boy to deal with."

"What do you mean, 'deal with'?"

"Hell, Currell, he's got to be killed! You ought to be able to see that if anybody can—it's your neck, and Chop-off's, on the line now!"

"I ain't going to kill no little boy, no matter what," Currell replied forcefully.

More pacing followed. Straker was in turmoil. He couldn't escape the ironic realization that Jimmy Rhoder, who had caused him such trouble in his life, now was about to cause him much more in his death. Rhoder had been murdered by lynching, at gunpoint, many days before in his own billiard hall by Straker. Straker had never been able to control his rage past a certain point, and Rhoder had unwisely pushed Straker far past the limit.

Straker's livelihood, beyond the generous allowance given him by his uncle Squire, depended upon the crime network he led. Small-time crime it was for the most part—foot-pad robberies, burglaries, prostitution, and some extortion—but it had proven profitable for Straker, who kept his little band of criminals in his grasp through gifts of money, women, and opium. Rhoder's mistake had been to believe he could compete with Straker and be allowed to get away with it. For a time Straker had put up with the growing competition, but when Rhoder tried to lure Straker's most effective footpads into his own fold, Straker decided matters had gone too far.

Straker had not really planned to kill Rhoder at first, just to scare him enough to persuade him to stick to the billiard-parlor business and leave crime to others. But matters got out of hand the night he paid his call on Rhoder's place, which had been temporarily closed because of damage from a fire. Rhoder was there alone that night, repainting a blackened wall, and before the night was over, he was hanging dead from a ceiling beam. Straker set the pool hall on fire again to destroy the incriminating corpse.

The fire, however, was doused before the job could be finished. Only through the help of Currell and Chop-off was Straker able to recover Rhoder's body and spirit it away before the murder was detected. Ample handfuls of cash had persuaded Currell and Chop-off to dispose of the body in the defunct mine belonging to Deverell.

The people of Leadville still wondered what had become of Jimmy Rhoder; most had finally concluded that he had fled town. At that point Straker ceased worrying much about the killing, but Chop-off and Currell continued to fret, fearing somehow the killing would be detected and their part in the cover-up exposed.

Then had come the much-talked-of death of Mickey Scarborough and the subsequent rumors about Briggs Garrett, and Straker had developed the plan that he hoped would be set in motion this very night.

Chop-off Johnson spoke up in his growly voice. "I'll be glad to kill the boy, Straker. I was for hunting him down and killing him before we come back here, but Currell wouldn't have anything to do with it."

Currell snapped, "Like I said, I won't be part of killing no boy. Ain't nobody going to believe his story anyway, now that Rhoder's body is gone."

Straker wheeled to face Currell, cursed him soundly again, then took a deep breath and forced himself to grow calm. He had always been proud of being able to work even accidental circumstances to his own advantage, to play whatever cards he was dealt. This was such a situation. Maybe he could salvage this situation yet . . . he had to, or his own neck might be on the line. "Both of you keep your mouths shut and let me think," he said to his underlings. "There's got to be a way out of this. Got to be."

He paced more, for a full five minutes, thinking over the situation. Finally he stopped. "If we're lucky," he said, "the boy will be too scared to talk. If he doesn't talk, this whole business will go no further, because nobody will believe Gunnison under the circumstances, and he never saw your faces in any case. You at least did one thing clever, Currell, when you pulled that whiskey trick. I'll give you credit for that.

"But if the O'Donovan boy talks, the law is bound to question you about it. If that happens, you're going to have to tell enough of the truth to be believable, but deny everything, absolutely everything, about there being any corpse in the mine. Your story will be that you were out near the mine, drinking together, and you saw Gunnison there, drunk and trying to hurt the boy. You went in to stop him, and Lundy got scared and ran. Gunnison fought you, fell down the shaft, and knocked himself cold. You got scared then, took him to town, and dumped him out in Stillborn Alley. That's that. Worst you'd get would be a lecture from a judge."

Currell said, "But what if they believe there was a body, no matter what we say?"

"They can't get anywhere on a murder case without the corpse on hand. You could say that this Gunnison was so raving drunk, he was seeing things. You could say he had the little boy so scared that he believed everything he said. The key will be to keep on denying, denying, denying. Like I said, there's nothing they could really prove without having the corpse. And likely it won't even go that far. With any luck, the boy will keep quiet out of fear."

"I don't like it," Currell muttered.

Straker grew angry again. "You don't like it? Then you should have run down the boy and killed him, and Gunnison too. Hell, if it came to it, you could have strung them up and burnt them and made them look like Garrett's victims too! But you didn't do that, and it's too late to change it. You put your foot in this one, Currell—put it in deep. You picked the wrong time to develop a high moral code!"

Straker turned and stalked to his horse. He mounted, looked at the others. "The worst part of it is that you've ruined my plan. But I'll fix it—there's always a way. I'll still make this town believe that Squire Deverell and Briggs Garrett are one and the same. I'll even still give you a cut of my inheritance, because I'm a generous man and because you did take a risk for me. But if you ever botch anything like this again, you're out. Understand? Cut out!"

Now it was Currell who grew angry. "Don't talk high and mighty to us, Straker! If me and Chop-off go down, you go with us! All we got to do is tell what you did to Jimmy Rhoder."

Straker shot a cold laugh back at Currell. "You think a jury would believe you above me? There's not a shred of evidence that would link me to any of this except your say-so, and that's not worth a handful of spit." With that, he clicked his tongue and rode off on a gallop toward town.

Chop-off Johnson watched Straker until he was gone in the darkness. "I ain't going to just sit still, whatever Straker says. You heard him just now—he ain't going to let this come back against him, no matter what. He'll leave us swinging in the wind, Currell."

The one-armed man looked south toward Chicken Hill. "That boy's got to be shut up, if it ain't too late."

Currell said, "No, Chop-off! He's just a boy, a kid..."

But Chop-off was already stalking away.

"Chop-off, don't do it!" Currell called.

Chop-off Johnson kept walking. Currell swiped a hand over his sweating brow. His throat was tight and dry. He lurched forward as if to go after Chop-off but pulled back, swallowed, and lunged back into his hut, locking the door behind him.

# Chapter 16

Chicken Hill was a well-populated extension of the larger Carbonate Hill, where several of Leadville's important mines were located. Primarily the domain of Swedes and Irishmen, Chicken Hill had been named for its first resident, William "Chicken Bill" Lovell, who had gained his nickname by trying to herd a flock of chickens across Mosquito Pass. The chickens froze to death on the mountain, but Chicken Bill delivered them down and sold them frozen to Leadville's winterbound miners, most of whom hadn't tasted chicken in months. The unusual feat only added to a colorful reputation he had started developing when he supposedly salted his Crysolite Mine over on Fryer Hill and sold it to the prominent H.A.W. Tabor. Tabor managed to turn the joke around by finding in it a high-yielding ore vein Bill had not known about.

Chicken Hill, like a homely woman, looked best in darkness. Cabins stood at all angles about the hill, and for every towering evergreen there were ten stumps, which created a hazard to Kenton and Gunnison as they wound their way through the farrago, wondering which cabin housed the O'Donovan family. Kenton ran into a stump hidden in the shadow of a cabin and swore.

Immediately a shutter flew open and a long rifle barrel protruded out at them, held by a bearded miner whose features were shadowed against the interior light of his cabin. They froze.

"And what do we be doing poking round out there?" said a very Swedish voice.

Kenton said, "Easy, my friend—I'm trying to find a particular residence to make a call."

"In the middle of the night? What kind of call would this be?"

"The circumstances are unusual," Kenton said.

"Yah, that I'd say they are," the man rejoined. There came a draining silence during which, Gunnison suspected, the man was considering whether to continue talking or just shoot the trespassers down and avoid the delay in getting back to bed. To Gunnison's relief, he kept talking. "Who yah be lookin' for?"

"The O'Donovan family," Kenton replied.

"Then why you botherin' us Swedes? The Irish live yonder." He waved with the rifle barrel.

"Which house?"

"That with the light still burnin'," the man said. "If you do them harm, my friends, all of Chicken Hill will be callin' in your debt."

"We mean them no harm," Kenton said. "Thank you, my friend. May I pay you for your guidance?"

"Indeed you may, thank you, sir." The rifle went, and an upturned hand came out in its place.

Kenton fished out a bill and handed it over. Then he and Gunnison turned and walked toward the O'Donovan house. The sound of the Swede's closing window drew a sigh of relief from Gunnison.

"I don't relish another gunpoint encounter like that," Kenton said as they rounded the front of the O'Donovan cabin. No sooner had he said it than the front door flew open and a woman with an older,

feminine version of Lundy's face and the wildest eyes
Gunnison had ever beheld leveled a rifle at Kenton's
nose.

"One twitch and you'll join the saints," she said.

Kenton and Gunnison lifted their hands toward the
black sky.

"Ma'am, please be careful with that weapon," Kenton
said. "We've come looking for Lundy O'Donovan."

At that, the woman gave a horrid screech and
raised the rifle higher. "What do you want with him?"
she demanded, almost in tears. "I'll see no harm done
my boy!"

"We don't want to harm him—we want to find
him, protect him if need be," Kenton said. "We are
concerned about him, afraid he's in trouble."

"Trouble?" The rifle lowered an inch or two. "What
do you mean by that?"

"My name is Brady Kenton. I'm associated with
*Gunnison's Illustrated American*. This is my partner,
Alex Gunnison. We gave Lundy some help yesterday
when some other boys were trying to take money from
him, and he wanted to repay us by showing us something he thought we would want to include in the
newspaper. He led Alex to an abandoned mine outside
of town and . . . it's a complicated story, Mrs. O'Donovan.
It would be much easier to tell without a rifle under our
noses."

She looked both intrigued and cautious, but after a
moment she bit her lip and lowered the rifle. "Lundy
spoke of meeting you, and said you paid him money for
something or another," she said. "Come in, then. If you
know aught about my Lundy, I'm wanting to hear it."

"He's not here, then?" Gunnison asked.

"Indeed he's not, and that's why I'm in the state I
am."

With the rifle lowered, Mrs. O'Donovan looked

about half a foot shorter than before and sad rather than maniacal. She stood aside to let the men enter the little shack, which consisted of three rooms: the main room into which they had just come, of which one corner was a kitchen, and two bedrooms, one off the side, the other off the rear.

"I've seen your name and picture in the *Illustrated American*, Mr. Kenton," she said wearily. "My husband, God rest him, liked you quite a lot."

"I'm gratified, then," Kenton said. "I'm sorry Mr. O'Donovan is gone."

"Aye, it's been hard it has. We've lost our first home to the lot jumpers and had to sell our little mine for lack of means to work it, but we get on with me taking in washing. But please, tell me about Lundy."

Gunnison took over the story, giving every detail, and what she heard clearly worried her. Tears began streaming down her face. "So it was a dead man he found!" she said. "Lundy told me he had found something important but wouldn't say aught of what it was. The boy likes his secrets too much. Oh, I wish he would come home so I could know he is well."

For Kenton's part, he was beginning to fear Lundy never would return, that whoever he had scuffled with at the mine, whether Briggs Garrett or someone else, had killed him. But the fact remained that Gunnison had not been killed and even had been dealt with mercifully at some difficulty. That alone gave hope that maybe Lundy also had been spared.

But there was a difference between Gunnison's circumstances and Lundy's that tempered the hope. Gunnison had seen no faces, heard no names. He had been unconscious when he was hauled up out of the shaft. Lundy, on the other hand, had probably seen who attacked him, maybe knew him, and that made him a threat that Gunnison was not. Kenton said nothing of this to Mrs. O'Donovan, seeing no value in worrying her more than she already was.

"Is there any place Lundy goes often other than here—a hiding place maybe?" he asked.

"Perhaps a thousand, for all I know. I'm so busy with my washing and the care of Old Papa that I mostly let Lundy run on his own."

"Old Papa, you say... would Lundy have told his grandfather things he might not have told you?"

"Aye, I believe he tells him all he knows, but it makes no difference. Old Papa is not right."

"Beg pardon?"

She tapped her head; the implication of mental disorder or injury was clear. "I can't tell you even to this day if he knows who I am. But I love him dear; Old Papa and Lundy and Mother Church are all I live for, now that my Jock is dead and buried. God has taken much, but left much as well in Old Papa and my fine lad." Then her face crumpled as she fought to hold back a sob, and Gunnison knew she had just realized again that her lad was not home.

"I wish I hadn't gone with him to the mine, Mrs. O'Donovan," Gunnison said, fighting back emotion. The stress of the long night was beginning to break him down. "Then none of this would have happened."

"'Tis not your fault," she said, wiping a tear on the back of her hand. "Lundy always finds trouble, with or without help."

At that moment, a dog snarled and barked at the back of the house; then there was a commotion, another bark, and the fearful yell of a man as something banged against the rear wall.

# Chapter 17

Kenton and Gunnison leapt up as one. "Check the back room!" Kenton ordered as he threw open the front door and went out, reaching under his coat for his Colt.

Gunnison drew his own Colt from under his jacket and bolted for the back room. Running to the window, he threw open the shutter and looked out. In the darkness there was wild movement, more barks and yells, and someone running away, obscured by darkness. The dog raced after him.

Kenton came around the side of the house. "There!" Gunnison shouted, and pointed in the direction the man had run. Kenton took off.

Turning, Gunnison started to run to the main room but stopped with a yell when he saw he was not alone. In the unlit room sat a man in a chair, weaving from side to side, one arm drawn up under his chin. Gunnison lifted his pistol before he realized this was the man Mrs. O'Donovan had called Old Papa.

"I'm sorry, sir," he mumbled, but Old Papa did not respond. He was not looking at Gunnison, and for all the young man could tell, could see and hear nothing. Seeing the shape the poor fellow was in roused in Gunnison a burst of new sympathy for the O'Donovan family and made him admire the resilient Mrs. O'Donovan for her dedication to caring for so unfortunate a man.

Gunnison went past the man and back to the main room, then out the front door into the night. Circling the house, he ran toward the place where the running man, the dog, and Kenton had vanished into the darkness.

Others were appearing, drawn by the stir and noise. "Who goes there!" yelled an Irishman.

"Trouble yonder!" Gunnison shouted, pointing ahead, then running on. The man followed. By the time he had gone another hundred feet, three others had come out to join the confused chase.

The dog was barking madly and making fighting snarls. They saw Kenton ahead. At almost that moment, there was the roar and flash of a pistol being discharged. It wasn't Kenton who had fired but the unknown party he was pursuing. The dog redoubled its clamoring. Kenton stumbled back as if he might have been struck.

"Kenton!" Gunnison shouted.

"I'm all right!" he yelled back. He ran farther into the night, and now Gunnison could see him no more.

The gunshot stirred the men with Gunnison to a frenzy but also made them fall back. Gunnison continued ahead alone, and one other faltered, then came after.

Ahead, Kenton again came into view, poised with pistol in hand, looking about. From the darkness another shot erupted. Kenton drew down and back as it rang. A slug slammed into the dirt at his feet.

Kenton lifted his Colt. It spat fire, and someone in the dark grunted and yelled. Mad scrambling followed. Kenton advanced, went out of view. In a few moments, he returned, pistol dangling at his side.

"Gone," he said. "Got clean away."

"Are you all right?"

"I am," he said. "Alex, I think I shot him."

* * *

Clance Sullivan stood silently in the corner of the office as City Marshal Pat Kelly leaned forward in his chair, Kenton seated across from him, very serious but calm despite the intense questioning to which he had been subjected. Having received the same, Gunnison had not done as well as Kenton and even now was dabbing nervous sweat from his forehead. The rising sun spilled in through the marshal's office window. It had been an amazingly long and busy night.

Gunnison had expected nothing good to come of this interrogation. The initial treatment given the journalists at the station had made him fear Kenton might face an assault charge. But now Kelly had a few cups of coffee down his gullet and seemed a touch more amiable than before.

By now, the entire story had been spilled, from the disappearing corpse to the absence of Lundy O'Donovan and the journalists' fears for his welfare. Clance Sullivan had told his story, too, and had surprised both Gunnison and Kenton by not seeming quite as antagonistic toward them as when he had left them at the abandoned mine.

Kelly stood and stretched, then paced in silence, thinking. Clance, Kenton, and Gunnison watched him expectantly. He had been in office only since April, having succeeded Martin Duggan, who had given Clance his job. Kenton had overheard somewhere that since Duggan's departure, crime had greatly worsened in Leadville, and there was talk among merchants and leading citizens of taking the law into hand more informally and violently.

Kelly faced Kenton and sat down on the corner of his desk. "Mr. Kenton, given that several witnesses say you were shot at before you fired, I'm not going to jail you. But don't think I believe all you and Mr. Gunnison are telling me. The story is a lot to swallow. Dead men don't get up and climb out of mine shafts, and killers don't soak citified young dandies in whiskey and dump them in Stillborn Alley."

Kelly looked Kenton in the eye as he continued. "I believe you are lying to me, and until I get to the bottom of this, I want both of you to remain in Leadville."

"We had no intention of leaving in any case," Kenton said. "Our intention is to do the work we came to do, and now, to find Lundy O'Donovan and make sure he's safe."

"I think you need not worry over Lundy. I know that little scamp; he's unsupervised and used to running about on his own, and likely will turn up presently with some explanation for his absence that's even more cock-and-bull than all you've told me. Lundy's full of imagination. Likely as not, he did tell you there was a body in that mine; it's not the first time he's spun tales and stirred up the gullible."

Kenton stirred in his chair and shot an acid glare at the marshal. Kelly saw he had Kenton's goat and obviously was gratified by it. "Here's what I think happened, Mr. Kenton. I think Lundy worked up a good story that prompted Gunnison here to go with him to that mine. Lundy's got no father now and likes attention from any man who'll give it. At the mine Gunnison took a tumble into the shaft and knocked himself cold. For all I know, he did honestly think he saw a dead body in that hole—a keen blow on the head can have you seeing angels and flying elephants and dancing girls on the rooftops. Lundy got scared that Gunnison had killed himself falling down the shaft, so he ran off to hide. He was afraid to come home, thinking somebody might have seen him with Gunnison and come looking for him after Gunnison's been gone awhile. In the meantime, Gunnison came around enough to climb out of that shaft, wander back to town, and head for a saloon, hoping to clear his head. He got good and drunk, passed out in Stillborn Alley, woke up, and staggered around the streets, and Officer Sullivan came along and found him. Once Gunnison was back in your company again, Mr. Kenton, he either dreamed up a story to cover himself for being drunk, or maybe he had heard the rumors about Briggs Garrett and was so addled, he convinced himself he really had found a burnt corpse of Garrett's trademark variety. You proved gullible enough to believe him, Mr. Kenton, and so rounded up Officer Sullivan again, went out to the mine, and of course found nothing.

"Officer Sullivan had the sense to know fact from make-believe and took his leave of you. But you weren't so quick to see the truth, and decided to go off looking for Lundy on Chicken Hill. You found his mother all stirred up because her boy hadn't come home, and convinced yourself even more that all the fantasies were true. Then somebody wandered by the O'Donovan place at the wrong time, got spooked by the dog and then by you when you tried to chase him down, and he went for his gun and led you to do the same. And now here we are. Make sense?"

He stopped and looked at Kenton almost smirkingly. Kenton just looked back at him and said, "May we go now?"

"In a few minutes, yes. But do stay close by. Shooting men in the dark is serious business, Mr. Kenton." An officer knocked on the door. "A moment, please," said Kelly. He went to the door, talked in whispers with the officer, then motioned for Sullivan to come with him. They went out, leaving Kenton and Gunnison alone.

After some silent moments, Gunnison asked, "Do you believe Kelly's explanation?"

Kenton looked at him. "Do you?"

"I admit it sounds like sense. It explains all the

facts without introducing disappearing dead bodies and long-dead outlaws stealing away little boys. The only trouble is, it isn't true. I know what I saw."

"And I believe you," Kenton answered. "Truth is a funny thing; it has twists and curves you wouldn't expect. It's sometimes not logical—any more than I am gullible. I resent him calling me that! Before this is done, I'll show that smirking jackass who's gullible!"

The office door opened again. Kelly walked in, a big smile of satisfaction on his face.

"Mrs. O'Donovan just paid us a call," he said. "She has Lundy with her. He came home on his own not an hour ago."

"Thank God," Gunnison said, scooting to the edge of his chair. "Now maybe I can get some vindication."

Kelly aimed his aggravating grin at him. "I'm afraid you'll be disappointed, Gunnison. It appears you're singing a solo in this particular choir."

"What do you mean?"

"Lundy says there was no body in that mine, that he didn't scuffle with anyone while you were in the shaft, and that he generally doesn't know what the devil you are talking about."

Gunnison sank back in his chair and felt like crying.

As the journalists returned to their apartment, Gunnison moaned in the pain of shattered credibility. He was now sure either Lundy had lied or that he himself was insane—and he wasn't eager to accept the latter alternative.

Kenton walked along with his head down, his brows lowered over his eyes. The wind made the brim of his hat wave and flutter as he listened to Gunnison complain. "Oh, cheer up, Alex! We'll get at the truth in the end," he said. "We're not going to sit on our rumps and let this go by. We're going to find the answer—and maybe Briggs Garrett in the process. If the man is alive, I intend to know it."

"That sketch in your room showing Garrett hanging the bridge burners—it had the detail of an eyewitness drawing," Gunnison said.

A moment of hesitation, then; "That's because it was an eyewitness drawing, Alex. I saw the whole sorry thing."

Suddenly Kenton's interest in coming to Leadville made a lot more sense to his partner. "So your search for Garrett is a personal one."

Kenton touched the scar across his cheek. "More personal than you know."

Alex wanted to learn more, but Kenton did not seem inclined to talk further and Gunnison was too bone-weary to press him. They stopped at a bakery and bought a loaf of bread, then reached the apartment, exhausted. It had been a long and strenuous night, so after a quick meal of sorts from the loaf, they retired. The sunlight pouring in around the edges of the window curtains did nothing to hamper their rest. Alex Gunnison slid into an oblivion almost as deep as that of the gruesome former human being he had fallen on in Deverell's mine shaft, and Kenton began snoring almost as soon as his body touched the bed.

# Chapter 18

For a long time, Gunnison's sleep was dreamless, but then he began to imagine himself in the scene Kenton had sketched. His hands were bound behind his back, a rope around his neck. Beside him were other men similarly situated. He was standing on the back of a flatbed wagon beneath the burned-out hull of what had been a railroad bridge.

Below stood a group of butternut-clad rebel soldiers, at their head a man with an uplifted saber. His face was featureless, like the face in Kenton's picture. He lifted the saber higher, then slashed it down, and the wagon beneath Gunnison's feet moved.

Suddenly Gunnison was swinging, his breath painfully cut off. Struggling for air, he kicked and flailed, pulled at his bonds, but found himself unable to break them. Through reddening eyes he saw one of the rebels coming to him, a bucket of coal oil in his hand. Liquid splashed on him, then the faceless man approached, his feet for some reason echoing loudly as they pounded the earth, and in his hand was a torch—

Gunnison awoke with a barely stifled shout, his pillow wet with sweat.

*   *   *

They had slept most of the day, exhausted from the harrowing events of the previous night. Gunnison ached from the physical punishment he had endured and felt emotionally drained. The afternoon was waning when the two journalists left their quarters and found a café where they quietly ate. Afterward, they walked through Leadville's crowded streets together, and for the first time Kenton opened up to Gunnison his wartime past and the background of his interest in Briggs Garrett.

"I knew Mickey Scarborough well in those days," he said. "We served the Union together, along with Victor Starlin, though not as regular soldiers. Espionage, infiltration, and sabotage beyond enemy lines was our specialty. It was all very secretive, directed through confidential channels, and I suppose that's most of the reason I have never told you about it. Confidentiality was pounded into us—we were never to reveal what we were doing, or for whom, no matter what the cost. Though we were directed by the government, officially we held no status, nothing to allow us to be traced. We knew that if we were captured, we were on our own, officially disavowed.

"Scarborough, Starlin, and I all had to deal with Briggs Garrett during the war. For Starlin and me, it was only one time, the time Garrett gave me this." He rubbed the scar on his face. "For Scarborough, there were three encounters; he knew Garrett far better than I did. Garrett left a scar on Scarborough just as he did on me, but a different sort of scar. His voice."

"So that's the secret behind that voice of his!" Gunnison exclaimed. He had heard of Scarborough's publicity device.

"Yes. His voice became like it was because at least once in his wretched life, Briggs Garrett failed to complete a lynching," Kenton said. "Scarborough's neck survived the snap, and Garrett was interrupted by the approach of a Union company before he could finish the task. But the noose had damaged Scarborough's throat. His voice was different." Kenton smiled faintly. "It was just like Scarborough to turn an injury to his advantage. But the fact is, Scarborough never forgave Garrett for what he did. It gave him a personal reason to see Garrett punished."

"No wonder he was so startled when he saw, or thought he saw, Garrett in his audience," Gunnison said.

"Yes, no wonder at all." Kenton paused somberly before continuing. "Scarborough and I had many different tasks during the war, including a lot of work across the line in Tennessee and down into Georgia, always posing as Confederate soldiers, renegades, or sympathizers. It was dangerous work in a war-divided region, but my Victoria's death was still fresh to me, and I frankly didn't care much what happened to me.

"The three of us smuggled counterfeit Confederate currency through Cumberland Gap to help weaken the rebel economy, sabotaged railroads, intercepted telegraph messages, even put on butternut-and-gray and mingled in with Confederate troops to pick up intelligence." Kenton chuckled. "Scarborough would even perform for rebel troops, posing as a traveling showman loyal to the South. Several times he and I came close to cashing in our chips, but we always pulled through.

"In those days, Garrett was a terror to Unionists on the Tennessee front. Led night riders, burned down farms and homes, murdered, assassinated. The South always officially disavowed him as a renegade, but intelligence showed he had ties to high-ranking leaders—he was, in effect, operating in a way similar to the way we ourselves operated, though he was far more vicious. He was an officially unofficial doer of the dirtiest jobs, the sort that didn't fit well into standard military practice. Some of that goes on in any war, Alex, and don't let anyone tell you otherwise.

"Starlin, Scarborough, and I were assigned back in sixty-two to head into East Tennessee and give assistance to a group of Unionist locals who were planning to burn some key bridges and hamper supply routes for Confederate supply and troop trains. The men had burned two on their own already, getting attention from as high up as the Confederate secretary of war. One bridge burner had been captured and hanged already, and the others were in great fear because word had come that Briggs Garrett was vowing to punish all bridge burners. Threats from Garrett were fearful things. He would stop at nothing and seemed unrestrained by any human compassion. We had received fairly reliable reports that he had torched Unionists' houses, knowing there were women and children inside and providing no opportunity for their escape.

"Starlin, Scarborough, and I joined the bridge burners, managed to destroy four more bridges without losing a man, and then came number five. We didn't know it, but Garrett was nearby with a small force. Our intelligence had failed us, and we proceeded to destroy the bridge. Garrett caught Scarborough and me. Only Starlin got clear. There was a battle around the burning bridge, two of our men killed. Garrett himself laid open my cheek with his saber, and I put a saber wound diagonally across his chest. There was a lot of confusion. I got a look at his face only for a moment, a poor look at that. If I saw his face today I wouldn't know it.

"Seven of our force were captured. Garrett executed them right there at the bridge. Hanged them, then doused them with coal oil and set them afire while they hung there. I've always hoped that none of them was still alive when Garrett set them all ablaze. God in heaven, a couple of those men were just boys, not even twenty years old." Kenton paused, looking away a moment or two before continuing. "I had passed out in some brush after taking the saber cut and saw it all after I came to. I had no weapon left; if I had, I would have found a way to rid the world of Garrett right there, no matter what the cost. Scarborough had been wounded and was unconscious through it all, hidden with me.

"Garrett left the bodies there. Examples, I suppose. Scarborough recovered from his wound and after that was determined to bring down Garrett. He never succeeded. A year after the bridge-burner hangings, Garrett got his hands on Scarborough and attempted to hang him, as I've told you before. Scarborough survived it, with that damaged voice.

"Garrett disappeared soon after. When the war ended, Scarborough went back to the stage, touring mostly in the West. We kept in touch occasionally, and I saw him while I was in California—he was performing in San Francisco. Then I lost touch . . . until all this happened."

"Ironic, in a way," Gunnison said. "It seems Garrett finally got Scarborough after all, just by showing himself and, well, startling him to death. And there's his other victim here, the one in the mine shaft."

"Yes . . . if in fact it was Garrett who did it, and Garrett who Scarborough saw," Kenton said.

"What are you saying?"

"That we still don't have any solid proof it was Garrett who killed the man you and Lundy found, or that it was really Garrett in Scarborough's audience."

"You said yourself that Scarborough would be unlikely to make a mistake about something that close to him."

"I know . . . but we have to consider every possibility. There might be something else going on here. There are so many questions. Take that corpse you found, for example. If Garrett is really alive, he surely is hiding his identity. Given that, why would he kill someone by his signature method, and then turn around and conceal the body? Garrett's way of killing was deliberately designed for show—he wanted his victims seen, not hidden. And there's still the question of why Garrett, if it was Garrett, would bother to haul you out of the shaft and dump you in Stillborn Alley rather than conveniently do you in. The pieces just don't fit like they should."

Silence followed, which was partly what made it so startling when gunfire abruptly erupted around the next corner. Shouts and screams followed. The crowded street began to clear. Kenton and Gunnison looked at each other in surprise, then Kenton said, "Lets go."

They approached the corner, falling in behind a uniformed officer who had just emerged from a saloon ahead of them.

# Chapter 19

The shooting had occurred at the doorway of a dance hall. An aged fellow who had apparently just emerged from the door had been shot down and lay moaning in a red puddle. Two policeman already had the apparent shootist, now disarmed, in their grip. Kenton saw that it was Smithfield, one of the men who had cornered him in the alleyway.

Recognizing Smithfield made Kenton's stomach gnarl. He suspected he knew the motive for the shooting, and a moment later his suspicion was confirmed when Smithfield, struggling against the grip of the officers, yelled loudly, "That's Garrett I've shot! Briggs Garrett!"

Kenton walked over and looked down at the wounded man, a tiny wiry figure who lay in the shaft of light coming from the dance-hall door that his own body was keeping propped open. Blood blubbered between purplish lips set in a graying face. This fellow was doomed.

Gunnison's eyes were big as he too looked at the wounded man for a moment until three others pushed in and knelt to try vainly to aid the other fellow.

"Kenton, could it really be Garrett?"

"Far too short and small, Alex. It's not Garrett."

"Kenton!" The yell came from one of the policemen

holding Smithfield. Kenton turned and saw it was Clance Sullivan. "You stay around a moment—I want to talk to you."

"Wonder what that's about?" Gunnison said quietly.

A third policeman arrived and took Sullivan's place as Smithfield was finally led away, still loudly and proudly declaring that he had killed Briggs Garrett. The wounded man, meanwhile, was being put into a wagon to be hauled off for medical care that would likely prove futile.

Sullivan dusted off his hands and walked up to Kenton. "Come take a walk with me," he said. "You'll want to know that I've changed my mind about the little incident at Deverell's mine."

They fell in side by side and strode down the boardwalk. "What do you mean?" Kenton asked.

"Just that I've come to believe Mr. Gunnison's story. I think there really was a body in that hole."

Gunnison felt a great wave of relief. "But what changed your mind?" he asked.

"Lundy O'Donovan."

"But Lundy denied everything I said!"

"Aye, and if ever I've seen a lying boy, it was Lundy O'Donovan. The poor lad was scared out of his head. Maybe Kelly couldn't see that, or didn't want to, but I could. As soon as he gave his tale, I knew he was shoveling the dirt over something. It's this old policeman's opinion that he was scared to do anything else."

"Scared . . . of whoever it was that Kenton shot at outside the cabin?"

"That's most likely."

"And do you think that whoever might have been Briggs Garrett?" Kenton asked.

Sullivan shrugged. "Who can say? Certainly there's plenty of others convinced Garrett is here. The one who just shot that old man back there, for instance."

"I suspected as much," Kenton said. "I wonder why he believed that poor devil was Garrett?"

"Because there's plenty of fingers starting to be pointed in this town. Somebody pointed theirs at old Walt Fisher, and this Smithfield found that enough reason to kill him. And it's a shame, it is, for I knew Fisher. He's no more Briggs Garrett than that tree yonder. He's just an old drunk who loitered about the dance halls to watch the women. I knew this sort of thing would begin soon. The Garrett talk is running too free."

"And what do you think of it?" Kenton asked. "Could there be truth to it?"

"As I said, who can say? You can be sure that Clance Sullivan will be keeping his eyes open, though."

Gunnison said, "I'm grateful you believe me. I was beginning to think nobody ever would, especially after the way Marshal Kelly talked to me."

"Kelly doesn't want to think Briggs Garrett could be in his town, and for that I can scarce blame him," Sullivan replied. "He knows that this sort of thing"—he waved back toward the dance hall—"can be the result."

George Currell took another mouthful of whiskey, his hand shaking so badly as he lifted the glass that he sloshed as much down his chin as he managed to swallow. He clunked down the glass, then again examined the loaded pistol on the table before him. It was the tenth time he had done this, for he was a man deeply afraid.

He had holed up in his cabin since the previous night, waiting for whatever would happen next. What that would be he could not begin to guess. He had initally expected Chop-off to return with the news that he had silenced the O'Donovan boy for good. When that had not happened within several hours, Currell's expectation had changed. It would be the law that showed up at his door, he anticipated, coming to arrest him for his part in all this. He thought about running but was afraid to. But the law had never come either.

In the afternoon he had removed his old army revolver from its case and loaded it, keeping it within easy reach. It gave him comfort, reducing his feeling of vulnerability. It did nothing for his mounting sense of guilt, however. He wished he had never agreed to help Mark Straker in his various criminal schemes, wished in particular he had not helped him cover up the murder of Jimmy Rhoder.

A noise outside made Currell stand with a loud gasp, shaking the table and overturning his bottle. Liquor spilled across the tabletop and the pistol. He righted the bottle and picked up the dripping weapon, then edged to his window and peered around the edge of the flour-sack curtain.

Outside, Mark Straker rode into the packed-dirt yard and dismounted. Even as Straker tethered his horse to a bush, Currell felt a wave of dreadful anticipation, fearing Straker was bearing bad news. He placed the pistol back on the table, took down his single lighted lantern from its nail peg, and went to the door. He opened it and stepped out.

Straker, approaching, looked Currell up and down in the lantern light. "You look terrible," said Straker.

Currell's only answer was silence.

"Have you heard what happened on Chicken Hill last night?" Straker asked.

"No. I been here all day."

"Somebody came poking around the O'Donovan cabin in the dark. Whoever it was picked a bad time to do it, though, because Brady Kenton and his partner were inside. Kenton came out . . . there was shooting. Kenton told the police he thought he hit whoever it was, but there's been no body found. Just a few splatters of blood. Either the wound wasn't fatal, or whoever received it didn't die until sometime later, someplace else."

Currell swallowed again and started to shake more. Despite his powerful build, he seemed little and weak. "How do you know all this?"

"There's a conveniently loose pair of lips at the police station." He was referring to a gossipy old fellow Kelly had retained to man the front desk and keep the office clean. Straker had discovered that a few little gifts of tobacco and cash would cause the man to tell everything he heard and saw at the station. The information had served Straker well many times, and the best part was, the old man was too imperceptive ever to question why Straker was so interested in police affairs.

"You think it was Chop-off?" Currell asked.

"I was going to ask you the same thing, Currell. Seems that I recall telling both of you to sit tight and leave the boy alone."

Currell was so nervous, he felt cold. "Chop-off said he wasn't going to sit and wait. Said he wanted the O'Donovan boy shut up for good."

"Chop-off's nowhere to be found today. Looks like it might be him who got shut up instead of the boy."

"The boy's all right?"

"You bet he is. In fact, he's already had a talk with the law. Gunnison has, too."

"Oh, no, no . . ."

Straker smiled without mirth. In his weakness, Currell seemed contemptible to him. "Don't worry yourself, Currell. The boy denied the whole story. Said there was no body in the mine at all and that he didn't know anything about what Gunnison was saying. The marshal believes Gunnison made it all up, or dreamed it while he was drunk."

Currell took that in for a moment. "So nobody's looking for me?"

"Nobody. You've got nothing to worry about now. And think about this: If Chop-off is dead, there's one less who knows what really happened. And Chop-off's shoulders provide a convenient spot for us to dump all the blame for Rhoder's murder if it ever comes back on us."

Currell grinned in comprehension. "Yeah. Yeah."

"So you can rest easier now."

"Yeah." Currell actually chuckled.

"Thought you'd want to know that, Currell. Also that my plan is going on despite the setback. Before long, all of Leadville is going to believe that Squire Deverell is not what he seems. And once he's gone, what he has is mine . . . you getting your cut, of course."

Currell chuckled again, but a thought arose. "But what about Mrs. Deverell?"

"What do you mean?"

"The inheritance would be hers first, wouldn't it?"

Straker grinned. "Not if she, say, poisoned herself in grief over the lynching of her husband. Such tragedies happen, you know."

Currell had no smile now. He was beginning to realize what a cold and frightening man young Mark Straker was.

"Good-bye for now, Currell," Straker said cheerfully. "You can put away your worrying now. And keep your eyes and ears open—soon the famous Mr. Brady Kenton will be heralding the 'truth' about Squire Deverell to the world."

Straker mounted and rode away.

Straker, riding back through the night toward the uneven line of flickering lights that was Leadville, thought to himself again how convenient it would be if

Chop-off was in fact dead, as he suspected he was. A dead man could never reveal the circumstances of Jimmy Rhoder's murder. Now only Straker himself and George Currell knew what had happened in Rhoder's billiard parlor that night.

How nice it would be, Straker thought, if Currell dissappeared just like Chop-off seemingly had. Why, perhaps the man might be found hanging from a rope, his body charred, providing even more proof that dastardly Briggs Garrett was at work even as he broke the last thread linking Straker to Rhoder.

Straker smiled to himself. The thought was nothing but a slightly playful consideration at the moment. It could always develop into something more, of course. It would depend partly on Currell's actions and attitude. Currell was weak. Too many lingering moral scruples. If he became a threat, he would have to be eliminated.

Straker began to whistle to himself. On the north edge of Leadville, two dogs began to fight, sending up fierce snarls and howls in the night.

# Chapter 20

Lundy O'Donovan woke with a shout, hands waving in the air. "Let me go!" he yelled. "Let me go!"

Across the dark room, Old Papa began writhing jerkily in his bed, responding to Lundy's cries. He made guttural sounds, and his right hand flailed, pounding the wall.

Into the room rushed Kate O'Donovan, freshly lit lamp in hand. Lundy had awakened by now and realized that he was only dreaming; he was sitting in his bed, staring toward Old Papa, who continued his movement and noisemaking.

"Papa, Papa, hush," said Kate O'Donovan. "Hush yourself now."

She sat on the edge of the bed, put the lamp on the floor at her feet, and placed her hand on the old man's forehead, gently pushing his bobbing head back onto the pillow. His flailing arm struck her hard in the side twice, but she did not heed the unintended blows. "Hush, Old Papa, it was only Lundy yelling in his dream. That's all."

Gradually the old man settled again. In a few moments his eyes closed. Kate O'Donovan looked at his face, smiled sadly and tenderly as she gave his brow a few more gentle strokes, then stood, picked up the lamp, and went to Lundy's bed. She sat down on it, put the lamp again on the floor, sighed, and looked for a long time at her son. "Lundy, it's time you spoke the truth to me," she said, whispering to avoid disturbing the old man further.

"I told you the truth," he replied, his eyes wide and gleaming in the light of the lamp.

"No, no you did not. I've known you from your first breath, my son, and I know when you are lying to me."

"I told the truth!" Lundy declared, more loudly. The old man murmured and stirred.

Kate O'Donovan put her hand on Lundy's. "What are you afraid of, son?"

"Nothing." Lundy smiled—obviously forced. "Why should I be afraid?"

"Why should some stranger approach our home in the night and fire a pistol when that Mr. Kenton went after him? Tell me that, Lundy. Did you see a thing someone didn't want seen? Was there really a dead man in the mine, like Mr. Gunnison said?"

Lundy's face looked thin and white. "I told you the truth," he said again.

Mrs. O'Donovan could see tears brimming on the lower rims of Lundy's eyes; he was struggling hard to keep them from overflowing. She said nothing else to him, just reached out and drew him close. She squeezed him, patted his shoulder, then had him lie down again. As she pulled the covers to his chin, she said, "When you feel ready to tell me the truth, then I am ready to hear it. You needn't be afraid to talk to me . . . and if there's danger to us, you must. Good night, Lundy. I love you."

"I love you too."

*     *     *

The sun, crossing the late-morning sky, illuminated the forms of two horsemen riding a southeastern route out of Leadville. The riders were Brady Kenton and Alex Gunnison.

They had rented horses at the James Stable, the same one that employed Perk as a watchman. Perk was not there at the time; he had worked the previous night, the stableman informed them. Perk was probably back home by now, he said, and that suited him. He didn't trust the scoundrel and had opposed his hiring. Perk Starlin, he said, would steal the coins off a dead man's eyes.

Kenton and Gunnison had ridden first to Chicken Hill, defying Kelly's orders to stay away from there. A uniformed officer was on the hill when they got there, which kept them from approaching the O'Donovan house but also was encouraging in that Kelly obviously had followed through with his pledge to keep an eye on the O'Donovans. "I wonder," said Kenton, "if Kelly doesn't give us more credence than he claims to. If he really believed the man I shot at night before last was some innocent straggler, he'd have me locked up and wouldn't be guarding the O'Donovans. I suspect this contrary attitude may have more to do with slowing down the local gossip mill than with his honest opinions."

"At least Clance Sullivan believes me now," Gunnison said.

"Others will be believing you too, before long," Kenton predicted. "What we have to find is a way to talk to Lundy O'Donovan and find out why he lied. My guess is the same as Sullivan's: it's fear. I don't doubt a moment that whoever he escaped from at Deverell's mine is one and the same with whoever it was I exchanged shots with on Chicken Hill. He came to kill Lundy, I'll bet you."

Kenton watched the officer a few moments longer,

then said, "Come on, Alex. Let's take a ride and see if we can find Perk Starlin's home. I want you to meet him. He's a useful sort of man to know in this town."

Getting out of town on such a beautiful day was pleasing and healing to Gunnison, who still suffered from the physical and mental bruises suffered in his unusual adventure. He relished the thin cool morning air, the vast blue of the sky, and the rocky splendor of the mountains all around. For the first time since his plunge into the mine shaft, Gunnison's mind felt completely clear.

They inquired of a man traveling toward Leadville and got specific directions to Perk Starlin's place, along with another comment about Perk's worthlessness and dishonesty.

They rode on, following the directions. Gunnison seemed more uncomfortable the closer they came. At last the cabin came in sight—a typically crude hut but a little larger than either man had expected.

"Do you think it's wise for us to be associating with a man with Perk Starlin's reputation?" Gunnison asked.

"I go by instinct, not gossip," Kenton said as the horses plodded toward the cabin. "I trust Perk Starlin."

No sooner were the words out than a rifle cracked on a nearby slope and a voice rang out: "That one was in the air, but the next will be in your vitals if you don't head on out!"

"Perk!" Kenton yelled, having recognized the voice. "It's Brady Kenton—don't shoot!"

"Kenton? Sweet mamma, why didn't you say so sooner?"

Gunnison took a long slow breath and let his heart descend from his throat to its usual location as the stout figure of Perk Starlin appeared from behind a tall boulder, smoking rifle cradled.

He scampered and slid down the slope and came

up to the mounted men with a big grin shining. "Kenton, I swear you ought to let a man know who you are before you ride down on his cabin like that."

"I'm not much in the habit of yelling my name like a fool when there's not a soul to be seen," Kenton said, beginning to dismount. Gunnison followed his lead.

"Alex Gunnison, meet Perk Starlin," Kenton said. The two shook hands.

"What were you doing up on the hill with a rifle, Perk? You pick people off on the road for fun or something?"

"Well, I had me some trouble with a fellow who claimed I stole a saddle—I heard he might try to find me if he could ever find out where I live, which is information I don't give out much. When I saw you coming, I thought you was him. Hey, what you gents doing out this way?"

"I wanted Alex here to meet you. And I was wondering if you had picked up anything new for me."

"Not a lot, not a lot. But I'm glad for the visit. You men dry or just empty?"

"Empty," Kenton said.

"You come to the right place," Perk said. "I'm loaded up with food—store-bought, too, fair and honest, and lots of it."

"How'd you come by the money?" Kenton asked.

"Sold me a saddle I happened to come by, that's all," Perk replied.

They ate their meal outside, seated on the ground. Kenton particularly enjoyed the bacon.

"Yeah, I heard about Smithfield and the shooting," Perk said around a mouthful of bakery bread. "Knew such as that would happen sooner or later. You get a town worked up over something, and somebody winds up using the situation to get somebody else hurt."

"I've been thinking the same myself," Kenton said. "Fear can always be manipulated."

"Well, somebody sure 'nough steered Smithfield the wrong way," Perk said. "The man he shot was sure not Briggs Garrett."

"Why's this Smithfield so interested in getting Briggs Garrett?" Gunnison asked.

"Glory," Perk said. "That's the goal of a lot of these fool young pistoleers—the glory of shooting down somebody big and famous. Talk is, Kenton, that the other one, Raglow, is still out gunning for Garrett. Too dumb to learn from what happened to his partner, I suppose."

The talk drifted to other subjects, and then sketch pads came out, and the journalists recorded both scene and scenery. By the time they mounted and headed back toward Leadville, Perk with them and heading for his job in the stables, a full day had passed. It had provided a welcome escape for Kenton and Gunnison from the intensity of their recent adventures.

The sun was a rich blob of orange light in the western sky when they reached the edge of town. The air was growing cooler.

# Chapter 21

Clance Sullivan wiped his fingers across his sweaty brow and noted blood on them when he pulled them away. "Ah, well, at least it's not my own," he muttered to himself, examining his fingers, then the drying blood-stains on his uniform.

It was going to be a rough night's duty—that he could see. Only two hours into the job, and he had already had to break up a knife fight and make three arrests. One of the bladesmen had drawn blood from another, splashing some on Sullivan. Though not squeamish, Sullivan disliked blood and particularly did not relish wearing it about on his garments. He shrugged. "Ah, well." There was certainly no time in the midst of a night's duty to change his uniform, even if he had a spare uniform to change into.

He pulled a handkerchief from his pocket and dabbed away the blood on his face, then folded the cloth carefully with the stains tucked inside, and replaced it in his pocket. At the same time he winced and moved his left shoulder in a circular motion—that pain again, radiating from his chest. The third such pain tonight, just like the pain he had experienced climbing up out of Deverell's mine. The pain brought with it a burst of perspiration. He wondered if maybe . . . no, no. He could not allow himself to think that.

Deliberately beginning to whistle, he strolled down East Third Street until he reached the intersection with Harrison, then turned left and proceeded for two blocks to Harrison's junction with State Street. For the next hour he worked that street, happily finding no more trouble.

Sullivan kept on whistling, and smiled and nodded at many people he passed, but inwardly he was troubled. In the air tonight was an aura of danger. Maybe all the Garrett rumors were getting to him, making him feel that any middle-aged male he encountered was potentially the "fiery hangman" of Civil War legend. Or maybe it was those troublesome pains in his chest. He remembered the day his father's heart had failed, like his father's before him. Again he pushed away the thought, unwilling to accept it.

Making another turn, Sullivan moved away from the crowded, brighter streets to Leadville's darker haunts. He slipped into the inky darkness at he end of an alleyway and leaned against a wall. Removing a paper from a pocket, he unfolded it and uncovered a half-smoked cigar. He lit it, illuminating the alley for a few moments, and drew rich smoke into his mouth. Shaking out the match, he continued walking. Sweat dripped from his eyebrows; his entire body was damp with it tonight.

Ahead loomed Jimmy Rhoder's burned-out pool hall. Sullivan wondered what had happened to Rhoder. The consensus seemed to be that the hot-tempered amusement merchant had torched his own building and left Leadville in anger, or that some competitor in business or crime—for the Leadville police well knew Rhoder's criminal activities—had put flame to the building and driven him away. No one had pursued the question very hard, for the police were glad to have Rhoder out of Leadville. He had been behind some of the growing footpad problem, though no one had ever been able to prove it.

Yet one thing mystified Sullivan. Since Rhoder's sudden disappearance, the crime problem had not significantly abated. If Rhoder had been a crime sponsor in Leadville, he apparently had not been that major a one. Marshal Kelly and his force knew that someone in town was supplying backing for a network of street thieves, burglars, and highwaymen—but whoever it was, he was hiding himself well. There were lots of theories about who it might be, and Sullivan had his own: Mark Straker.

Sullivan had never trusted Straker. All his peace-officer instincts spoke against the man. It was well known that Straker received a generous allowance from his uncle Squire Deverell in return for no work at all—this despite Deverell's obvious dislike of his nephew—but it always seemed to Sullivan that Straker was usually too flush for even a large allowance to account for. And he kept bad company. Perhaps Straker was the man behind the scenes of much of Leadville's crime; perhaps it had been he who had somehow gotten rid of competitor Jimmy Rhoder.

Sullivan's thoughts were jarred by movement at the far end of the alley beside Rhoder's building. Most likely it was a dog or other varmint digging through rubbish, but he decided to check it out, having nothing else to do at the moment. Sliding quietly into the alley, Sullivan crept through the darkness toward the rear of the burned building.

He froze when into a beam of moonlight stepped a figure. No varmint, this one—at least no animal varmint. It was Chop-off Johnson, covered with grit and ash, holding a little metal box he had apparently dug from the rubble of the pool hall. Standing quietly, Sullivan watched Chop-off kneel and force open the box, then smile as he found what appeared to be a pipe and quantity of smoking opium. Rhoder's, probably. Chop-off must have come foraging in hopes of finding such a prize. Chop-off pocketed his find and threw the box aside.

Sullivan was about to step forward and make himself known when Chop-off stood again and took a clumsy step. Sullivan only then noticed the blood-crusted bandage around the footpad's leg. Chop-off took a few more steps; he was limping. Sullivan developed a suspicion so strong it felt like certainty: Chop-off Johnson was the unidentified interloper shot by Brady Kenton behind the O'Donovan house on Chicken Hill.

Now, that was intriguing. Sullivan's mind began piecing together possibilities. If Chop-off had come to find Lundy, then it must have been he whom Lundy had seen at the mine, who dragged Alex Gunnison out of the shaft and dumped him in Stillborn Alley, who had removed the burned body Gunnison had described . . .

Burned body . . . Sullivan glanced over at the fire-ravaged poolhall, a new idea springing to life. Could the body have been Rhoder's? It was pure speculation, but certainly a possibility.

Chop-off limped away, heading for the nearby edge of town, marked by a line of brush and trees. Sullivan followed in silence. Chop-off entered a narrow pathway through the brush. Sullivan paused a few moments, then did the same. It was dark here, and he had to pick his way slowly to avoid making noise or tripping. He certainly didn't want Chop-off Johnson to detect him in such an enclosed dark place. Sullivan's heart began to pound heavily. Another stab of pain came, halting him in his tracks. It was stronger this time, and he wondered if he should go on or turn back and seek help.

After a few moments, the pain subsided, and he chose to go on. He wanted to see where Chop-off had gone, then interrogate him. The pains he would simply ignore . . . just a strained muscle, that's all.

Coming out on the other side of the line of brush, he saw Chop-off limping across a barren rising expanse near the entrance of a mine. Probably the one-armed scoundrel had himself a shed or lean-to up there somewhere. Chop-off continued up the expanse, reaching its crest and crossing over. The policeman followed, the climb seeming unusually difficult. His heart hammered so loudly, he could actually hear it. He sweated all the more, and by the time he reached the spot that Chop-off had crossed; he could no longer deny that something was seriously wrong.

Sullivan stopped, his face drenched and white. Before him stood Chop-off Johnson, facing him squarely. "Why you following me, you damn lawdog?" the footpad demanded.

Sullivan stared at him, his heart still pounding unusually hard and hurting like the very devil.

Chop-off limped forward, drew back his single fist, and struck him, the blow knocking Sullivan on his rump. "I don't like being followed," Chop-off said. He kicked the policeman in the forehead.

As he fell back, Sullivan felt something like an explosion in his chest, followed by a terrible wrenching pain. He did not much feel the impact of Chop-off's kick, for darkness was wrapping around him like a shroud, a shroud that was far too tight across the chest. And then, strangest thing, he saw the entire scene from above: Chop-off standing there in the moonlight, single fist clenched, and his own form, lying on the ground and looking up, eyes half shut.

Then it all receded, rushing away at a fantastic speed until it was gone.

Mary Deverell wiped her eyes quickly, seeming embarrassed to be crying in front of another human being. Weeping, her stern husband had often preached, was a sign of weakness in both men and women.

Nevertheless, given what she had just been told by Mark Straker, the woman could not restrain the tears from flowing down her deeply lined cheeks. She leaned over in her chair, put her face in her hands, and wept so hard that her narrow shoulders shook. Straker, seated across from her, had been watching her with an expression of great sympathy while she was looking at him; now that her eyes were downturned, he watched her with cold satisfaction.

At length Mary Deverell forced herself to stop crying and sat up straight again, lifting her damp and reddened eyes to meet the gaze of her husband's nephew. "I'm sorry," she said shakily. "This is such terrible news . . . how could he do this to Squire? He seemed like a nice man."

"Brady Kenton is no nice man, Aunt Mary. Far from it. He came to Leadville determined to find Briggs Garrett, and he'll not leave until he's pinned his tag on someone. And it seems like that someone, unfortunately, is going to be Uncle Squire."

"But it's a lie!"

"I doubt Kenton cares. He just wants his story, no matter what the cost to another man's reputation and safety."

The woman looked afraid. " 'Safety' . . . what do you mean?"

"Briggs Garrett is a hated man, Aunt Mary. Already, one man in this town has been shot to death by a gunman who wanted the honor of killing Briggs Garrett.

But it wasn't Garrett he killed, just some poor old man he thought was him."

Mary Deverell's eyes widened as realization set in. "So if Brady Kenton says that my Squire is really Briggs Garrett, someone might believe him and—"

"A lot of people will believe him. The man has credibility—even Uncle Squire swears by him. Of course, Uncle Squire doesn't yet know what Kenton is doing to him."

"He hasn't written his story yet, has he? Oh, say he hasn't!"

"He hasn't. But he's starting to talk. Right now, the rumor hasn't gone far, from what I can tell, but I don't doubt that before tomorrow night, every saloon in Leadville will be filled with men telling their neighbors that they've just heard, on the good authority of Brady Kenton, that Squire Deverell is really Briggs Garrett."

"They might hurt my Squire, Mark!" She began to weep again. "We've got to wake Squire and tell him what's happening!"

Straker reached up to dab his eye. He was enjoying this sham—and his aunt was reacting just as he'd intended she should. "Don't worry, Aunt Mary," he said. "And don't bother Uncle Squire with this. He's not as young as he used to be, you know, and he might not bear up well under such a shock. I can take care of Kenton. I'll go over first thing tomorrow and publicly confront him and make him recant his story. Then I'll toss him and his partner right out of those rooms. It's absurd that Uncle Squire should be giving free lodging to a man who's determined to do him wrong."

Mary Deverell smiled through her tears and put her thin hand on Straker's. "Oh, Mark, what would I do without you? You're wise and good."

"Aunt Mary, don't you worry—I'll take care of this scoundrel Brady Kenton."

"Thank you. Good night, dear Mark. You're so good to me!"

"That's because I love you, Aunt Mary. Now, you sleep. I'll stay down here tonight, on the couch, so you can know I'm close."

Mark Straker leaned over and kissed Mary Deverell's wrinkled cheek.

# Chapter 22

Chop-off Johnson sat in a crouch, panting for breath, his back against a mine building. The uniformed body of Clance Sullivan was stretched out before him. He had just dragged the policeman's limp corpse to this hidden place, out of the moonlight, for fear someone might see both it and him. He couldn't imagine why the policeman had died—he hadn't hit or kicked him all that hard . . . had he?

Anyway, the man surely was dead, and all Chop-off could think about was that maybe somebody else had seen the policeman following him out of Leadville. If so, he would surely be blamed for the death once the officer's body was found. Chop-off felt a great wave of fright. He was in deep enough trouble already, given his failure to eliminate Lundy O'Donovan. To make it worse, he had even taken a bullet wound in the leg from that big man who had emerged from the cabin and chased him. It was just a grazing wound, but a painful one that had festered. Afterward, Chop-off had run away and hidden himself in a forgotten old hut up here in the woods behind this mine, imagining that all the world was out there trying to find and punish him.

Only the craving for more opium to dull the pain in his
leg and the rising panic had driven him out.

What could he do? He was afraid simply to leave
the policeman's body. He needed either to get rid of it,
as he and Currell had gotten rid of Jimmy Rhoder's
decaying remains, or to make it look as if someone else
were responsible for the death. How could he do it? He
wished he were as smart as Mark Straker, who always
seemed to find a safe and clever way out of his
predicaments.

The thought of Mark Straker brought a fast,
heartening inspiration. Why not borrow the idea Straker
had planned to use to make Rhoder's murder look like
the work of Garrett? Of course! Smiling, Chop-off stood,
peered around carefully to be sure no one was within
view, and slipped around to the front of the building
behind which the body lay. The moon was irritatingly
bright at the moment, spilling a dim glow across the
rugged countryside and the never-sleeping town just
over the hill. Chop-off eyed the mine's main building
about three hundred yards to the east; if there was a
watchman, he probably was there. Sidling against the
front of the immediate building, he peered through a
window. Though it was too dark to see much, he could
make out various bundles, crates, kegs, and the like
inside. This was some sort of warehouse. If he was
lucky, it would contain what he needed.

Chop-off picked up a stone, wrapped the tail of his
ragged jacket around it, and as quietly as possible
shattered one of the windowpanes. Reaching in, he
unlatched the window and slid it open.

Inside, after a frenzy of match-lit searching, he
finally found what he hoped for: a length of rope and a
keg of coal oil. He checked out the window before
tossing the goods out, then, seeing a desk beneath the

next window, had a fresh inspiration. Rummaging quickly through it, he found a pencil.

Once outside again, he closed the window and carried his take around to Clance Sullivan's body. Chop-off's leg hurt terribly, and he longed for opium. No time now, though. He dragged Sullivan closer to the back of the warehouse where a beam and pulley jutted out above a closed double door on the upper level.

Pausing just long enough to catch his breath, the footpad went back around, brought up his keg and rope, then sat down, screwing up his face in discomfort as he bent his wounded leg. So far, his plan was working. No one had appeared, no watchman had shouted at him. Taking up an end of the rope, he wondered briefly how one tied a hangman's noose, then realized he probably couldn't tie one with one hand even if he knew how. It would have to be a simple slipknot, the kind he could make one-handed.

It took him longer than he'd thought it would to tie the knot and loop it around Sullivan's neck. A flight of steps led up to the closed upper-level doors, and this Chop-off mounted, reaching the loading platform from which he was just able to reach the pulley and thread the other end of the rope through it. He worked it down until it reached the ground, then descended the stairs again.

He spilled coal oil over the form of Clance Sullivan, picked up the end of the rope he had just passed through the pulley, and said, "Up you go."

With a groan, a heave, and a screeching of the pulley, he strained over toward a nearby tree, in the process hefting up Sullivan's body until it dangled two feet off the ground. Straining to keep his grip, he wrapped the rope around the tree several times, then managed to tie it off. The knot was loose but sufficient.

Now sweating and breathless, Chop-off limped back

to the corpse and dug into his pocket for a match. Just
as he was about to strike it, he remembered the inspiration that had come in the warehouse. He pulled out the
pencil stub, picked up a piece of plank from a nearby
pile of scrapwood, and scratched out four words. Tossing
the pencil away, he placed the plank upright against a
stone near the swinging body.

"Now they'll be sure to say he done this to you,"
Chop-off said in a half-whisper, addressing the corpse.
"Got to light you up now, policeman." He smiled. "And
then I'll go back to Chicken Hill and use the rest of my
coal oil, just in case that boy ain't talked yet after all."

He struck the match.

# Chapter 23

Brady Kenton and Alex Gunnison were simultaneously awakened in their apartment by the clanging of a fire wagon passing on the street. Both rose, met wordlessly in the hall, and walked to the front window.

A fiery glow rose in the sky to the east. Both journalists watched in silence a few moments, and then Kenton said, "Alex—that fire is on Chicken Hill."

"You think . . ."

"I don't know. And I don't like not knowing. Let's go."

They dressed in a rush. By the time they reached the street, a sizable crowd was already heading toward the fire. A couple of quick inquiries confirmed Kenton's suspicion that the fire was on Chicken Hill, reportedly at the O'Donovan cabin.

"It appears Kelly's policemen didn't do quite the guard job needed," Kenton said grimly.

By the time the journalists reached Chicken Hill, flames were spitting skyward in big orange tongues, licking out of the windows and door of the cabin that had been home to the O'Donovans. Firemen were pouring water on the fire, but it was clear they could hope to do no more than keep the flames from spreading to other structures. The house was lost.

"I hope...they got out," Kenton said, panting from his run.

"Look there," Gunnison said, pointing. Silhouetted against the flames were Lundy and his mother, both hugged up against the sad old grandfather, who was seated in a big wicker chair that apparently had been saved from the fire. A handful of other possessions lay about them, the total making a pitiful pile there on the hillside. Another pile was heaped nearby; it was laundry. Mrs. O'Donovan, honest Irish laundress that she was, had thought of her customers and saved their clothing, probably at the expense of losing some of her own goods.

"How did it start?" Kenton asked a man beside him.

"Don't know for sure, but I heard it was set deliberate," he said.

"By who?"

"Durned if I know." The man moved away, backing off from the roasting heat that belched out in all directions around the burning house.

"Come on," Kenton said. "I want to talk to Mrs. O'Donovan."

They came upon them from the rear. Kenton called her name. Kate O'Donovan and Lundy turned. Tears were streaming down their faces as for the second time in their life in Leadville, a home was taken from them. The first loss had been to lot jumpers—ruffians who took advantage of Leadville's property laws by forcing residents off property and building a new structure on it, giving them title. Now arsonists had victimized the O'Donovans.

Lundy's expression was intensely fearful. He pulled back behind his mother's soot-smudged skirt as the journalists approached.

"Who did this to you?" Kenton asked Kate O'Donovan.

"Faith, if I knew, I would tell," she said.

Kenton knelt and looked into Lundy's face. The boy's tears streamed down faster; he was unable to hold Kenton's gaze.

"I'll bet you know, don't you, Lundy?" Kenton said.

Lundy buried his face in his mother's skirt and cried harder.

"Do not push the boy now," Mrs. O'Donovan said. "He's much afraid."

"So I see."

"I thank the Savior that we are alive," she said. "A roof over one's head can be found again; the life of a boy and an old man cannot be."

"Very true," Kenton said. He looked at Lundy again. "Son, I won't press you, but if you have withheld anything that needs telling, you'd best speak before there's even more loss."

Kate O'Donovan exclaimed, "Mr. Kenton, please do leave him be for now!"

The old grandfather stirred in his chair and made a guttural sound, staring as an infant might at the fire, seeing but not comprehending. Moving colors, ravaging heat. To him, that was all it was.

Kenton said, "Mrs. O'Donovan, I just can't leave it be right now. You realize that whoever set your house afire probably was trying to kill Lundy. Lundy knows something someone doesn't want known, even though Lundy has been too scared to say it. Am I right, son?"

Gunnison watched out of the corner of his eye as Lundy finally nodded.

"Do you know who set the house on fire, Lundy?"

"I think I do." The last time Gunnison had heard Lundy's voice, it had been screaming, sounding quite different from the quiet near-whisper it was now.

"Did this same man attack you at the mine?"

"Yes."

"Who?"

Tears gushed anew. "I'm afraid," he said. "He'll kill me if I tell. He'll kill Old Papa and Mama."

"You've got to tell us, Lundy. It's important we know. This man let you get away from him one time, and also spared the life of Alex here—but apparently he has changed his mind. It's not just your safety and your family's at issue anymore—it's Alex's as well."

When Kenton said that, Gunnison's stomach rolled over twice, like a trick dog upon command. He could not restrain himself from asking his own question then: "Lundy, was it Briggs Garrett?"

Lundy shook his head. "It was a man with one arm," he said.

Gunnison was so surprised, he sank to his haunches on the ground. "Chop-off Johnson? It was Chop-off Johnson who attacked us at that mine?"

"I don't know his name. I've seen him before in town. There was another man at the mine with him, too. Somebody I've seen, but I don't know his name."

"I had wondered how a one-armed man could have gotten a corpse and an unconscious man out of that shaft all alone," Kenton said. He paused, thinking. "If it was Johnson who was poking about your house last night, then he surely has a bullet in him. I shot at him, and I hit him. Lundy, when you saw the one-armed man tonight, did he look wounded?"

"He had a bandage on his leg," Lundy said. "I saw it when he set fire to the house."

"You actually saw him torch your house?" Gunnison asked.

Lundy nodded. "He threw coal oil or something on the wall, then a torch. I was too scared to yell until it was already burning. It's all my fault."

"Nonsense," Kenton said. "Don't even think that. Lundy, listen: We've got to go talk to the law. Chop-off Johnson needs to be in jail."

Gunnison rose from his crouch. "Look," he said, grasping Kenton's arm and pointing.

There, barely visible in the circle of light cast by the flaming house, was a dark and familiar figure. He had only one arm and was creeping away from the scene.

"You there!" Kenton yelled. "Hold it right where you are!" Kenton began trotting toward him.

Chop-off Johnson saw him coming, turned, and ran.

Gunnison commanded his legs to move, but they would not. Like Lundy, he was paralyzed with fear of the one-armed man. Only after Kenton had vanished into the dark did Gunnison snap out of the spell and go after him.

Across Chicken Hill Gunnison ran, looking in all directions, but he could not find Kenton or Johnson. It seemed impossible they could have gotten away so quickly, but then he realized that once out of view, the pair could have gone in any direction. Suddenly the dark cabins around, empty because all the occupants were at the fire, seemed ghostly and threatening. Around any of their corners Chop-off Johnson might be lurking, ready to kill should Gunnison come too close. His first encounter with the man came back clearly—the long blade of the footpad's knife and his attempt to disembowel him.

Gunnison wanted to shout for Kenton but was afraid to. Moving slowly now, carefully, he advanced, looking all around as he went. The wind sang around the houses and in the treetops. Voices and the clatter and ruckus of fire fighting carried down from the direction of the O'Donovan place. Gunnison's pistol was heavy in its holster. Could he use it if need be? Gunnison had never shot at a man before. Tonight he might have to.

"Kenton?" It was a whisper rather than a shout, for he feared shouting. No answer returned.

On he went, looking, seeing nothing, yet feeling through some innate sense that Kenton and Johnson had come this way.

Then suddenly he knew he was not alone.

"Gunnison?"

He recognized the voice at once. "Currell? Is that you?"

"What's happening up there?" George Currell asked.

"Fire at the O'Donovan place. Set by Chop-off Johnson."

There was a long silence. "He's alive, then," Currell said in a flat tone, almost as if he were disappointed. "He's just been hiding out, that's all."

"What are you talking about?"

"Nothing, nothing—just shut up and leave me alone!" Currell sounded distressed and defensive—a sudden transformation. He turned and dashed away into the night.

Feeling suspicious, Gunnison wondered if he should go after Currell and leave Chop-off to Kenton. He decided he could not do that; he had to know his partner was safe.

Movement in the darkness ahead. He bolted forward.

The moon was a come-and-go light in the sky, and the clouds that had blocked it for the last several moments let it shine through now. There was Kenton, pistol drawn, running around the corner of a shed below. Here there were houses, sheds, outbuildings, stockpens, chicken coops. The rears of houses and commercial structures were ugly there in the uncertain moonlight—Leadville with its trousers dropped.

Gunnison was already bearing down on the place he had seen Kenton before it hit him that he should be more cautious. Chop-off Johnson was probably armed. The excitement of the chase and his concern for Kenton had so overtaken Gunnison that he had forgotten common sense. He pulled back into the thick nightshadow beside a woodshed.

The back door of the closest house opened, and a shirtless man in trousers and galluses came out with a shotgun. He peered around in the dark, stooped over a little, like a farmer looking for foxes in his henhouse. Gunnison hugged back against the shed.

The man with the shotgun stared directly at him, but Gunnison could not tell if he'd been seen. Moonlight washed over the shotgun bearer, but Gunnison remained in the shadows. The man looked from side to side. At last he shook his head and reentered his house.

Gunnison waited a few moments—sure enough, the curtain in the nearest window moved; the man was still watching. After a time there was no more such movement, and Gunnison felt safe in moving again.

In all this time Gunnison had heard nothing to indicate where Kenton and Chop-off might have gone. He had lost precious time just now.

Gunnison slipped away from the woodshed, and as quietly as he could, left the backlot and got onto a small alley street running parallel to the backsides of a row of buildings. Music from a nearby saloon rippled on the breeze. He advanced. A dark alley opened to his right, and he let it swallow him.

Halfway down the alley, he again felt the presence of another. "Kenton?" he said.

A moment later, he knew it was not Kenton. A figure materialized before him, almost invisible in the blackness. A cool metallic surface brushed his arm, and a pricking knifepoint stung his skin.

"Money." This was a to-the-point footpad.

Gunnison backed away from him. His hand went beneath his coat, and he grasped his pistol.

The footpad slashed at him. "Money!"

"I'm getting it for you," Gunnison said. Then he drew the pistol and swung it. Metal pounded skull, and the footpad went down, shuddering all the way. Gunnison stepped across him to continue down the alley.

Around the corner, a hand caught him from the side and pulled him down. The moon sailed out from behind another cloud and threw a thin ray down into the alley. It caught Chop-off's ugly grin and glinted on his uplifted pistol.

"Now I'll do what should have been done back at that mine," he said. The moon sailed behind another cloud.

The roar of the shot was deafening—but then, Gunnison's pistol had always had a noisy report, and the closeness of the alley made it even louder. Chop-off's scream joined the echo of the shot. Suddenly he was there no more.

Gunnison pushed up and looked for him, but Chop-off, like the burned corpse in the mine, had strangely vanished. Gunnison wondered if his shot had struck Chop-off or just scared him off.

Kenton . . . where was he? Perhaps Chop-off had evaded him. Or perhaps . . .

Fighting back fear that was starting to catch up with recklessness, Gunnison lifted his pistol, wondering if he should go after Chop-off or look around for Kenton . . . or Kenton's corpse.

In the dark ahead something bumped about. Chop-off maybe, or Kenton. Gunnison wanted to run away but would not. Instead he continued, pistol lifted.

# Chapter 24

Chop-off Johnson came upon Gunnison suddenly, from the side as before. He had put away his pistol and drawn his long knife. It cut a thin swath across the back of Gunnison's hand, and Gunnison's pistol slammed hard against a wall beside him. He almost dropped it.

Somehow Gunnison managed blindly to grab the single wrist. Enraged, Chop-off bellowed, sending out bursts of foul breath.

If he had possessed two arms, Chop-off likely would have killed Gunnison on the spot. As it was, as long as the younger man held his arm tightly, he could do little but writhe, kick, and try to bite, which he did with much vigor and swearing. Hot blood splattered Gunnison's face.

"I don't want to kill you!" Gunnison said with a straining voice. "Give it up—I've still got my gun!"

Chop-off let out a yell and kicked Gunnison's feet from beneath him. He went down as cleanly as a soldier fainting at attention. Gunnison's pistol came up. He squared it on the one-armed man and pulled the trigger.

Nothing happened. Jammed. The pistol must have been damaged when it hit the wall.

Gunnison felt a sharp sting as Chop-off's knife

147

grazed over his shoulder. He had aimed for the heart, but Gunnison had twisted enough to make him miss. Rolling to the side, Gunnison freed himself and bounded to his feet to begin a blind run.

Chop-off was directly behind, amazingly fleet for a wound-crippled man. This way and that Gunnison darted, until suddenly he realized Chop-off was no longer on his heels. He stopped to catch his breath and saw he was beside a long ladder leaned against the side of a two-story building. Without a second thought, he climbed it, feeling he would be safer above the street than on it. When he reached the roof, he pulled the ladder up, making more of a clatter than he wanted to. He hoped Chop-off had fled.

A look around revealed that the building he was on was fire-damaged; the smell of ash and charred timbers was strong. Though he did not know it, by chance he had stumbled upon Jimmy Rhoder's pool hall; the ladder in the alley had been used in battling the fire. Part of the roof ahead of him was gone.

*At least up here Chop-off probably won't spot me,* Gunnison thought. *I'm safe for now. I can wait out the night if need be.*

He worried about Kenton. What if Chop-off had killed him? Kenton was not the kind just to give up on a chase, yet he was nowhere to be seen.

Winded, Gunnison sank to his haunches and breathed the cool Leadville breeze. It chilled the sweat clinging to him and made him shiver. Moonlight beamed out again, causing him to feel exposed, so he moved more to the center of the flat rooftop. There he fumbled with the pistol, trying to unjam it, but it was no use.

Time went by. He heard no worrisome sounds from below. Chop-off Johnson was surely gone.

The man's persistence in attempting to kill him frightened Gunnison. It also confused him, for he still could not understand why, if Chop-off wanted him dead, he had passed up the best opportunity to be rid of him in Deverell's old mine. Something must have changed his mind. Chop-off had obviously seen this chance encounter as an opportunity too tempting to pass up.

Or perhaps something or someone else had restrained Chop-off from violence at the mine. Lundy had said there was a second man there. As he sat on the charred rooftop, Gunnison wondered if the second man might have been George Currell. He and Chop-off did seem to have some connection, and Currell had acted peculiarly enough tonight to make Gunnison suspect he had some hand in all of this.

Something scuffed on the roof of the adjacent building. Gunnison stood and turned in one motion.

Chop-off stood on the edge of that roof. He was looking squarely at Gunnison. "Time for you to die," he said, lifting his pistol. He fired a shot that sang past Gunnison's ear, then another that clipped away part of his collar. When Chop-off pulled the trigger a third time, the pistol merely clicked. It was empty.

Chop-off swore loudly, threw down the gun, and leapt the gap between the buildings, going for his knife.

Gunnison, panicking, backed away as Chop-off approached, but there was no escape. Chop-off closed in, his knife went up, and Gunnison did the only thing possible—jumped through the burned-out portion in the roof nearby and into the dark building below.

Perhaps Gunnison was stunned by the drop, for after it came a small gap in memory that he was never able to fill. The next thing he was aware of was pushing up to a squat. A big hole gaped above, sky showing through. He had fallen only one level, to the second floor, which was badly burned and a few feet from him sagged down into emptiness.

Gunnison clambered to his feet and felt dizzy. He tripped over a pile of sticks on the floor and almost fell. A quick look showed the sticks to be a bundle of fire-damaged pool cues. He picked up one of them. It was comfortingly stout, a useful club should he need it.

Looking up, Gunnison waited for Chop-off to appear at the edge of the hole. He did not.

The young journalist crept to a side window and looked out. Two men passed below in the alley. Maybe a pair of footpads, or maybe policemen—he couldn't tell from this angle.

Chop-off dropped through the hole and immediately came at him, his knife ready.

Gunnison let out a yell to the strangers below: "Help me! Murder!"

The next moments consisted of dodging, ducking, fighting as best he could. He swung the billiard cue back and forth, which kept Chop-off at enough distance to keep him from using his long knife for the moment. Gunnison would not be able to keep him off forever, though. Chop-off was obviously determined to see him dead.

Gunnison decided to try to reason with his attacker. "Killing me will do you no good," he said. "Lundy O'Donovan got out of that fire. You didn't get him. He's already admitted there was a body in that mine, after all, and that you were there. He's talking to Marshal Kelly right now." Gunnison didn't know if the latter statement was true, but he hoped Chop-off would think so.

Chop-off paused, breathing even harder than before. "I can't take the chance you're lying to me," he said. "I've got to go ahead and kill you, just in case." He shifted the knife and advanced.

Gunnison swung the cue just as the charred floor-board beneath his right foot gave way and his leg went through, up to the thigh. He was painfully trapped.

Chop-off laughed. He put his knife between his teeth and came forward, nimbly grabbing the pool stick and wrenching it away. He took the knife from between his teeth. "You'll slice up pretty as a Christmas goose."

The knife descended. Gunnison gave a desperate wrench, trying to pull his caught leg free, and at that moment a gunshot echoed through the empty building.

Chop-off's head jerked to the side, and he fell directly before his intended victim, dead eyes staring into Gunnison's in the moonlight, his knife still gripped in his single hand.

# Chapter 25

"Alex!"

Kenton came bounding through the doorway, preceded by a young policeman with a smoking pistol in hand. Kenton ran to Gunnison and pulled him up and free. The policeman went to Chop-off's body and stared down at it. Now Gunnison knew who the two passersby below the window had been.

"Alex, thank God you're alive!" Kenton said.

"I've never killed anyone before," the policeman said, still staring at the corpse.

"He would have killed me," Gunnison said. "You did what you had to do."

The earlier gunfire and general tumult had drawn attention, and now others entered the building and climbed the stairs. Gunnison explained what had happened as best he could and then was quickly hustled off to Kelly's office along with Kenton and the young officer who had saved Gunnison's life. The officer, Kenton would later explain, had come along at the most fortuitous moment, having responded to Gunnison's gunshot in the alley when Chop-off had first attacked. Kenton had lost Chop-off's trail sometime before and was desperately trying to regain it when he and the officer met. They heard Gunnison's cry from the window and entered the vacant building just in time to save his life.

Kelly was surprisingly calm, given his earlier attitude toward Kenton and Gunnison. He questioned Gunnison closely, then Kenton, and finally the officer, and when it was done, seemed satisfied that what had happened was an honest case of police action to halt a murder.

Kelly sat down on the edge of his desk and revealed why his attitude had softened. "I talked to Lundy O'Donovan a few minutes ago. He's reversed his story. He's now backing up what you said, Mr. Gunnison. He says there was a body in the mine. He said he had found it even before he took you to it. Lundy also told me that he was attacked at the mine by Chop-off Johnson, and that there was another man there, too. He said he lied because he was afraid the men would hurt him and his family if he told the truth."

"Was the second man George Currell?" Gunnison asked. Both Kenton and Kelly reacted with surprise.

"We suspect so . . . but how did you know?"

"I saw Currell tonight, right after Kenton took off after Johnson. I was only with him a few moments, but the things he said, the way he acted—I suspected he had been involved."

"Alex, maybe you're learning to think like a good journalist at last," Kenton said in a tone of admiration.

"Please, Mr. Kenton, let me do the talking," Kelly said gruffly. "Did you see where Currell went?" he asked Gunnison.

"No—he ran off into the dark. He seemed very upset to learn that Chop-off had started the fire. And it was strange . . . he acted unpleasantly surprised to find out Chop-off was even alive. I didn't really understand it all."

"Well, maybe soon we'll have answers for you. We're looking for Currell right now," Kelly said. "Lundy couldn't identify him for us, but we know Currell and Chop-off Johnson ran together some. Now that Johnson is dead, Currell may be the only way to finding out if there is anyone else behind all this."

"Briggs Garrett, perhaps?" Kenton said.

"Mr. Kenton, I instructed you to be quiet," Kelly snapped. "But since you mentioned it, yes, I must consider the possibility that the Briggs Garrett rumors might have a factual basis. Given the fire tonight, and this shooting death, this town is going to absolutely blow up with more speculation. People here are eager to believe that Briggs Garrett is alive and up to his old tricks, and believe it they will. It's going to behoove me and my men to try to either disprove or verify all these blasted rumors, and if they are true, to find Garrett and put him into custody. Otherwise we'll just have more innocent people being hurt or killed, like that poor old man who got shot down outside that dance hall."

"Marshal, may I ask one more question?" Kenton said.

Kelly looked perturbed, then shrugged. "Go ahead."

"Is the O'Donovan family safe? If there really is someone—Garrett or otherwise—pulling the strings from the background, Lundy could still be in danger."

"The family is safe," Kelly replied. "We've found someone with the space and means to take them in, and no, I won't tell you who it is, because I don't want you poking around them. In fact, Mr. Kenton, I still hold your presence here largely responsible for perpetuating these rumors."

"You have a right to your opinion."

Kelly stretched and yawned. He had gotten only a

little sleep before the night's ruckus broke loose. "And what about you, Mr. Gunnison?" he asked. "Do you feel the need for police protection?"

"I think I can take care of myself," said Gunnison.

"I feel the same," Kenton replied.

"I didn't ask you, Kenton, in case you didn't notice," Kelly said. "Very well, Gunnison—it's your choice. But let me warn you both: I catch you in the middle of any more trouble, and you'll find new quarters in my jail."

The door opened, and an officer thrust in his head. "The O'Donovans are ready to go, Marshal."

"Hmm? Oh, yes. Send them on, then." The officer nodded and started to withdraw, but as an afterthought Kelly asked, "Where's Sullivan? I haven't seen him since I came in."

The officer shrugged. "No one else has either, Marshal. I'd been wondering about him myself."

"He'll turn up, I guess, and he'll have a talking-to due him when he does. I don't like my men making themselves scarce when things are busy."

The officer withdrew. Kelly yawned and stretched again. "What a job," he muttered. He waved toward the door. "You two get on out—I've had my fill of you for tonight."

When they had left the station, Kenton said, "You know, for some reason, I'm beginning to like Kelly, in a way."

"Now I know you've gone loco on me," Gunnison replied. "He's one of the harshest coots I've run across."

"Yes, but at least he knows you're no liar now . . . Alex! Look there."

Kenton indicated a large carriage that had just pulled around the side of the station, drawn by an impeccably groomed chestnut horse. In the driver's

seat was the most distinguished-looking black man
Gunnison had ever seen. He wore formal clothing and
sported a headful of thick graying curls, closely cropped.
At first, Gunnison's eyes were drawn mostly to the
driver, but as the carriage turned and clattered off, he
saw a face peering out from behind the drawn curtains.

"That was Lundy O'Donovan!" Kenton said. "And
I'll bet the seat of my pants that that driver is taking the
O'Donovans to wherever it is they'll be put up. And I
admit, I'd like to know where that is. It could be useful.
Besides, I like the idea of knowing something Kelly
doesn't want me to."

"Shall we follow?" Gunnison asked, hoping the
answer would be no, for he was longing to return to his
bed.

The answer, of course, was yes, so Gunnison found
himself trotting along in the street, trying to keep the
carriage within view. It made a turn ahead, and Kenton
pulled him into an alley, shortcutting to the next street.
So their course continued for a few minutes until at last
they saw the carriage pulling into a driveway beside a
familiar tall house on Chestnut Street.

"Kenton, that's the same house where I saw the
girl looking out of the upper window," Gunnison said.
He was half afraid to say it, for he remembered the
obvious pain the subject had caused Kenton before.

"Yes—but even more interesting than that, Alex—
look at the name on the door."

Gunnison drew closer, squinted. "'Chrisman.'
Kenton, isn't that—"

"The same house where Mickey Scarborough died?
Indeed it is."

"Well, this Chrisman woman must be a generous
sort, taking in Scarborough and then the O'Donovans
too."

"It would seem so, wouldn't it?" Kenton replied.

"Well, let's get back to our quarters again, and maybe get a little rest before the new day comes bearing down on us." He patted Gunnison's shoulder. "Quite some exciting nights you've had lately, Alex. Our Leadville trip is one you'll never forget."

"If I live through it, I'm going to do my best to try," Gunnison muttered.

He and Kenton turned and walked away together.

# Chapter 26

The man's name was Shapiro, and in the morning light he reminded Mark Straker of a sallow weasel. Straker had roused the fellow from his cot in the corner several minutes before, having arrived long before the opening of the posted business hours. His earliness was deliberate, for he wanted this transaction to be private and undisturbed.

Shapiro was sitting in a printing office as disheveled as himself. Straker wondered how a business this new could have managed to grow this dirty. He sat cleaning his nails as Shapiro read the handful of script-covered foolscap he had given him several moments earlier. As Shapiro finished the last sheet, Straker leaned back and yawned. He had been up late the previous night, ostensibly "guarding" the Deverells but actually writing what he now felt was quite a good piece of work.

Shapiro put down the pages and scratched his head with a spider-leg finger. Remarkably thin, Shapiro was rumpled and tousled; his wiry dark hair, clipped short, stood up straight on his head. Straker had to swallow a chuckle when it struck him that with hair so stiffly upright, Shapiro could make a sideline income renting his head out as a horse brush. Judging from the ratty filthiness of the man's topknot, he could almost believe Shapiro had done just that.

"Where'd you get this?" the printer asked.

"That doesn't matter. The question is how quickly you can print it for me. The author wants it on a single page, like a broadside, so he can display it around town."

"The 'author,' huh? Who's the author?"

"He wished to remain anonymous."

"I can see why." He picked up the sheets again. "If I read this right, it sounds like he's saying that this here—" he scanned for the name that was escaping him, "this here Squire Deverell is really Briggs Garrett!"

"I don't really want to comment on what it says. My assignment was just to bring this down here and have five hundred copies printed, as quickly as possible."

Shapiro read the title on the top sheet. "'Confession of a Traveling Journalist.' Interesting." He smiled slyly. "Hey, I bet I know who you are!" he said. "You're the partner of that Brady Kenton, ain't you! The *Illustrated American*! I heard Kenton and a younger fellow are in town. Kenton wrote this, didn't he!"

Straker deliberately fidgeted, letting his manner answer the question affirmatively while saying, "I really can't say any more."

"Hah! I knew it! But I got a question. If Kenton wants this published, why not just put it in the *Illustrated American*?"

"There are some matters too, well, controversial for a publication of that type. There are time factors to be considered, too, when the information is as crucial as this. Brady says he . . ." He put on the expression of a man who has just realized he has said too much. "Never mind that. Don't take any of that as a confirmation of your speculations."

Shapiro's eyes glittered. "Yeah, yeah. All right. I

don't know a thing." He slapped the back of his hand onto the papers. "You know, this could be dangerous to me if I printed it."

"I see no reason it should have to bear the printer's name, do you? There are other shops in town—no one will know who did it. You can deny it along with all the others. Anyway, I think you have a moral obligation to help get this information before the public."

"Well, I do have a backlog to consider, too. Other jobs lined up and waiting, you know."

Straker didn't believe that for a moment. He knew that Shapiro had been open only a week and had printed no more than one stack of shoddy-looking hand-bills for a dance hall. Straker had picked up saloon intelligence about Shapiro, checking him out for this job, and knew he was as ratty in heart as he was in grooming. Shapiro had come to Leadville fresh after being fired from a printshop in Denver. Rumor had it the firing offense was suspected theft of a spare press, probably the very one now set up at the rear of this seedy one-room operation.

Reaching into his pocket, Straker pulled out a roll of bills and placed them on top of the foolscap. "Perhaps this could persuade you to make this job your top priority," he said.

Shapiro's spidery fingers wrapped around the bills and pulled them into his palm. "I believe that will take care of the problem."

"Good, good."

"I can have the broadsides by, say, tomorrow afternoon."

Straker shook his head. "No. Tonight."

"Tonight! I can't possibly—" He glanced at the bills in his hand, then nodded. "All right. Tonight. When will you be by to pick them up?"

"I won't be. All you need to do is put the loose

stack on a rooftop somewhere where the wind can hit it. That will do an ample job of distribution."

Shapiro looked amazed. "You want these printed and thrown to the wind?"

"What better way to spread them anonymously? And I suggest you make sure no one sees you with these."

"Yeah. All right. I'll do it . . . but I've got to warn you: It won't take anybody long to figure out that it's Brady Kenton who wrote this."

Straker had now stood. "Oh my, do you think so?" he said in a very sincere tone. He headed for the door, turning his back on Shapiro. When his face was hidden, he smiled. "I surely hope you're wrong about that, Mr. Shapiro."

The knock echoed through the empty store building below Kenton and Gunnison's rooms. Kenton put down his notepad upon which he had been writing furiously and stood.

"Maybe it's Perk, come to give us some news," he said as he and Gunnison descended the interior staircase.

It wasn't Perk, though, but a tall and well-dressed black man. Gunnison thought he seemed familiar and realized all at once that this was the man who had driven the O'Donovan family from the police station to the Chrisman house in that curtained carriage.

"Mr. Kenton, sir, my name is Gableman," he said in a deep, creamy voice. "I'm sorry if I've disturbed you, but my employer has asked me to deliver you this." He handed Kenton a gilt-edged envelope. "It's an invitation to diner this evening," he said. "Mrs. Chrisman is a longtime admirer of the *Illustrated American*, and your work in particular, sir, and did not want you to depart Leadville without paying a call, if you will."

Kenton opened and read the neat little invitation

card. "You may tell Mrs. Chrisman that we will be glad
to attend."

" 'We'?" Gunnison said.

"Yes—the invitation includes you . . . see?" He handed
the card to Gunnison.

"Mrs. Chrisman will be pleased, sir," Gableman
said. "I'll leave you gentlemen to your business now,
and look forward to your visit tonight. Thank you." He
gave a polite little dip of his long chin and turned
toward the street, which was rapidly filling with Leadville's
morning traffic.

At that moment a voice rang out from somewhere
on the street: "Kenton! Brady Kenton!"

"What the—"

"Damn you, Kenton, come out here and face your
accuser like a man!" the same voice cried. Now its
source came into view through the bustle of people,
almost all of whom now had stopped to observe what
was happening.

"That's Mrs. Deverell's nephew, isn't it?" Kenton
asked Gunnison without taking his eye off the approaching
young man.

"Yes—Straker I think his name is."

Straker's face was red and his voice tight with
seeming fury. He stopped about ten feet away from
Kenton and spread his stance wide. A finger came up
and shook toward Kenton's face.

Gableman, who looked very unsettled but no less
dignified, quietly stepped back. This was not his affair.

"Kenton, who the hell do you think you are,
spreading what you've been spreading?" Straker demanded in a voice loud enough for everyone within a
block to hear.

"I don't know what you're talking about," Kenton
calmly replied.

"I think you do, Mr. Kenton, I think you do. I've

heard it from a dozen different places now—you're spreading it across all Leadville that my uncle Squire is Briggs Garrett!"

Kenton, seldom surprised by anything, was now surprised beyond words. "What? Deverell—I never . . . not once have I . . ."

Gunnison, who was praying that the apparently furious Mark Straker had not come bearing weapons, looked around at the crowd. From at least a score of expressions he could tell that Straker's remarkable accusation had been clearly heard by all of them. People began to whisper. Some backed away. Others drew nearer.

"My uncle Squire has been generous to you in allowing you free lodging in his own rooms, and you repay it by accusing him in alleys and back rooms of being Garrett—damn your betraying soul, Kenton, I should have you arrested!"

"I've never made such an accusation about your uncle," Kenton said. "Blast it, the thought hasn't even crossed my mind!"

"Liar!" Straker shouted. "Liar! I know what you've been saying! Everyone knows!"

Kenton was again too taken aback to complete a sentence. Straker stepped forward. "Out! Out of these quarters, right now! You'll not stay another moment under Squire Deverell's roof!"

Kenton's face was red, and his pulses throbbed visibly in his temples. "Very well," he said. "We'll be out within five minutes, though I question whether you have the right to force us out."

"Out! Or I'll snap your neck with my own hands!"

Kenton wheeled, then stopped. He turned again to face the crowd of people now gathered near the porch upon which he stood. "Hear me!" he called loudly. "This man doesn't know me, or know what he's talking

about. I'm no barroom gossipmonger. I don't spread
rumors. When Brady Kenton makes accusations, he
doesn't do it in alleyway whispers, he does it in print—
and with the facts to back it up."

Straker's expression became even more angry, but
inwardly he felt a rise of joy: Kenton could not have
picked more self-damaging words, as Kenton himself
would soon enough realize.

Kenton said to Gunnison, "Come on, Alex. Let's
gather our things."

"Sir," Gableman said, stepping in from the side.

"Yes?" Kenton sounded angry, but Gableman
apparently knew the anger was not directed at himself
and did not seem to take offense.

"I think I can tell you with reasonable assurance
that Mrs. Chrisman will be glad to store your possessions for you until you can find new lodging. In fact, sir,
she may be able to help you even on that latter score."

Kenton raised his brows. "Mrs. Chrisman seems to
be a particularly helpful woman."

"Oh, she is, sir, she is."

Straker gave a final call. "Get moving, Kenton. I
want you out of there right now!"

Kenton's face again went crimson. "You'll have
cause to regret this, Straker!" he shouted. Wheeling,
he walked back into the building and toward the stairs.
Gunnison followed.

"That sounded an awful lot like a threat, Kenton,"
Gunnison said. "Do you think you should have said it?"

"Probably not, Alex. But my temper got the best of
me, and what's said is said. Come on—let's get packing.
I want to get out of here."

# Chapter 27

Gableman was still outside when Kenton and Alex emerged. Straker was gone, but clumps of people remained, talking among themselves and looking with great interest at Kenton when he reappeared.

One man approached. "Mr. Kenton, my name is Allen, with the *Lake County Reveille*. I overheard the exchange a few minutes ago. Have you anything to say about Mr. Straker's charges?"

"I don't think yelling on the street should receive the honor of being called 'charges,' Mr. Allen. And as I said earlier, I don't make back-room accusations. Anything I have to say I will say in print, when the time is right."

"In the *Illustrated American*, you mean?"

"I don't want to talk any more about it, sir. Good day to you."

Allen touched his hat. "Thank you, Mr. Kenton. If you ever wish to say more, please call on me." He turned and walked away.

Gableman stepped forward. "If you'll allow me, Mr. Kenton. I'll carry your bags for you."

"No need, Gableman—I can handle them well

enough. I hope our coming will be no imposition on Mrs. Chrisman."

"I think she will be glad to see you, sir."

They walked together toward Chestnut Street. As they were about to round a corner, another yell reached them.

"Kenton! Kenton! Wait!"

Kenton grimaced. "Not again!" he said beneath his breath as he turned.

This time it wasn't Straker or a newspaperman but Perk Starlin. He pounded up, breathing hard, his face flushed. "Kenton, I'm durned glad I saw you. You got to come."

"What is it, Perk?"

"This will take a little while, in case you're doing something else," Perk said. He let his eyes flit over to Gableman and back again. The message was clear.

Kenton turned to the black man. "Gableman, would you mind going on without us? I've seen Mrs. Chrisman's house, so we can easily find it later."

"Very well, sir. When can we expect you?"

"I honesty don't know."

"Then at your convenience will be fine. As I said, I have no doubt Mrs. Chrisman will accommodate you now that you're without shelter." Gableman took the bags, said his good-bye, and walked away.

"Who was that?" Perk asked.

"His name is Gableman. He's a butler for Ella Chrisman."

"Ella Chrisman! How did she come into things? And what did he mean by you being without shelter?"

"I'll explain all that, but first I want to know what's got you so worked up."

Perk glanced around and spoke surreptitiously. "The police are trying to keep it quiet, but there was a hanging and burning last night."

"What?"

"You heard me right. Up behind a mine storehouse just outside town. A man strung up to a pulley beam and set ablaze. The fire burnt the rope in two, and he fell. The mine watchman never saw a thing when it happened, but at first light he found the corpse all heaped up and smoking. And when he kicked him over, you'll never guess what was under him." Perk paused dramatically.

"Go on, Perk, go on!"

"A sign, handwrit on a piece of board. It said Briggs Garrett done the hanging. The police is all in a dither over it, and not just because of the sign and all. The man who was hung was Clance Sullivan."

Kenton and Gunnison looked at each other in horror. "Are you sure, Perk?"

"I just came from the very spot myself—I was there even before the police were. I know that watchman, you see, and I was the first he told when he found the body. I went up and seen it, then took off before the police come around."

"They're still there?"

"Indeed they are."

"Take us there, then. Or at least tell us the way."

"Come on—I'll get you close enough to find it and let you go on up alone. I don't go around much where policemen are."

Marshal Kelly glared in displeasure when he saw Brady Kenton and Alex Gunnison coming around the corner of the mine storehouse. He stomped over and cut them off.

"Who the devil steered you up here?" he demanded.

"Never mind that. Is that Clance Sullivan's body lying yonder?" Kenton asked.

"Now it's my turn to tell you to never mind. Turn your tail and get out of here, both of you!"

"Come on, Kelly. Let us try to help you. We've been cooperative with you so far, haven't we?"

Kelly glowered at Kenton in silence, then sighed deeply. "What does it matter? You've already seen it now. Come on—if your stomach's not too weak."

Gunnison could hardly bear to look at the blackened remains that had been Clance Sullivan.

Kenton stared at the still-smoking corpse wordlessly, a grim expression on his face. "Do you have a theory as to who did this, or why?" Kenton asked Kelly.

"Are you asking that for publication, or your own information?"

"The latter."

"Well, I don't know why I should tell you anything at all, but . . . here. Take a look at this."

He stepped up and took something from one of the three pale-faced officers. He handed it to Kenton.

It was a board. On it was scratched the following: *DONE BY BRIGS GARRAT.*

"Interesting," Kenton said.

"Disturbing is more to the point," Kelly replied. "I can hardly doubt now that Briggs Garrett is alive, after all."

Kenton shook his head. "If alive he is, that board certainly doesn't prove it."

"What do you mean?"

"Briggs Garrett, I happen to know, was a reasonably educated man. He knew how to spell his own name at the very least." He waved over at the corpse. "And he also knew how to tie a proper hangman's noose. I can see from here that the knot yonder is only a slipknot."

"So what are you saying?"

"That whoever did this was certainly not Briggs

Garrett. It was someone trying to cover his guilt by making it appear that Garrett did it."

Kelly thought that over. "Perhaps you're right, Kenton. But it's hardly going to matter if word of this gets out. All of Leadville will take this as final proof that Briggs Garrett is alive and killing again, just like he did in the war."

"Word, I'm afraid, will get out," Kenton said.

Kelly faced him with a frown. "Is that some sort of threat?"

"No—just an observation. Take a look." Kenton pointed toward a clump of brush behind which a group of boys hid, watching the entire scene from only a dozen yards away.

"Hey, you boys!" Kelly shouted. "Come out of there!"

Come out they did, but they did not linger. They turned on their heels and scampered away.

Kelly swore and stomped his feet. "Now," he said, "all hell really will break loose."


The woman was one of those fortunate few who had not lost beauty along with youth. She sat in a small room, her eyes fixed on a face in a portrait hanging on the wall before her. Her lips were tightly shut, the pressure whitening the skin immediately around them. A soft knock on the door of the little room caused her to look away from the portrait a moment, but her eyes returned to it as she said, "Come in."

Gableman entered. "I did as you asked, Mrs. Chrisman. Mr. Kenton accepted your invitation very readily."

"Good," she said. "Thank you, Gableman. I'm eager to hear whatever he has to say."

"There were some events that happened while I was with Mr. Kenton that you need to know of. I took a liberty I hope you will find acceptable." Gableman succinctly described what had happened between Mark Straker and Kenton, and his tentative offer of lodging for the journalists.

"You presumed correctly, Gableman," Ella Chrisman said. "It would be useful indeed to have Mr. Kenton and his associate under this roof. Tell me—did Kenton deny the things this Straker man said about Squire Deverell?"

"Not directly. He said only that any accusations he made would be in print. Of course, I didn't question him myself."

"Of course. Perhaps I'll be able to clarify the matter with him personally. Where is he now?"

"He and his partner were called aside by a man while we were coming here. I don't know what the business was, but it seemed urgent, and the two of them left with him."

"I see. I'll have to be patient, then. And patient I can afford to be, as long as I've waited." She stared more deeply at the portrait. "I can feel it, Gableman—a great sense of anticipation. Answers are coming that I've wanted so many years now. At last I'm going to know the truth."

"Yes, ma'am." Gableman watched her a moment as she stared at the portrait on the wall. When he saw a tear roll down her cheek, he looked away.

"I'll leave you alone now, Mrs. Chrisman."

"I'm not alone," she said. "I'm never alone when I'm with my Jerome."

"Yes, ma'am. Of course." Gableman turned and left the room.

# Chapter 28

Mary Deverell was struggling hard to avoid becoming either angry or hysterical with her husband. "You must listen to me!" she said, stepping in front of him to block him from reaching the door. Outside, the sun was edging westward. "It's no longer safe for you to go out, not after what Brady Kenton has done to you!"

"Brady Kenton's done nothing, and your nephew's words to the contrary don't mean a thing. You're foolish to trust Mark so much, Mary. You don't know him for what he really is."

"He's a good boy, Squire—it's you who's wrong about him, not me. If he wasn't a good boy, why would he have warned us about Kenton?"

"Because he's a born liar. Mary, if Brady Kenton had been going around telling people I was really Briggs Garrett, you think I wouldn't have heard of it by now? I don't know what sort of trick Mark is trying to pull, but a trick it is, I assure you. Now, I've gone along with your worrying and fretting all day, but I've got business that needs doing over at Number Three"—the reference was to his newest mine—"and Willie will be gone from there within an hour. So let me pass, woman!"

Mary Deverell's wrinkled face fell, but she stepped aside. "Please, Squire, be careful."

"I'm always careful," he replied, pulling aside his lightweight riding coat to reveal the Remington holstered beneath it. He left the house and trotted lightly down to the street.

"Uncle Squire!" Mark Straker's voice came around the corner of the building. He had just descended from his upstairs quarters. "You shouldn't be leaving alone— let me go with you."

"I'd sooner have the devil by my side," Deverell snapped. "Come to think of it, there would be little enough difference."

"Please let Mark go with you," Mary Deverell pleaded from the door.

"No—let him stay here. Protect you from all the gunfighters and bugaboos supposedly coming to get me."

Straker, a sad expression on his face, walked up to his aunt's side and took her hand, watching as Deverell rounded the house on the opposite side, heading for his stable. "I do wish he wouldn't be so stubborn," Straker said. "And I wish he would give me more of a chance. I've never understood why he dislikes me so. Sometimes I think the only reason he lets me stay is that you care for me, Aunt Mary."

"Squire's a hard man," she answered. "Someday he'll appreciate you. I know he will."

Deverell came riding back around the house on his favorite chestnut mare. He glanced over at his wife and Straker as he passed, his sour feelings toward the younger man evident in his expression. An evening wind gusted through, sending the dust that Deverell's mare kicked up blowing down the street. Straker's quick eye caught something else blowing in that breeze—a broad sheet of paper, printed on one side.

"Let's get you inside, Aunt Mary," he said. "I'll be right in and stay with you until Uncle Squire gets back."

Mary Deverell, ever obedient to her beloved nephew, entered the house. Straker waited until she was well inside, then darted over and caught the blowing paper. He turned it over and by dusklight read the freshly printed title that spread across the top: *CONFESSION OF A TRAVELING JOURNALIST*.

Straker smiled. Shapiro had done his job well. Carefully folding the broadside, he tucked it under his shirt and headed back toward the Deverell house.

Squire Deverell usually enjoyed riding in the wind, but this evening there was something different in the restless atmosphere. The road out to the Number Three seemed lonely and long, and the darkening sky lowered Deverell's spirits. Maybe it was all Mary's keening and fretting affecting him, Deverell speculated. Maybe it was the vague chance that Mark had been telling the truth about Brady Kenton's alleged storytelling.

Deverell did not know that Straker had evicted Kenton and Gunnison from the quarters he had lent them; Straker had urged his aunt to say nothing of it yet in light of Deverell's obvious admiration of Kenton. So it was that Deverell was considering the possibility of riding back home by way of the new store building and asking Kenton man-to-man about Mark Straker's talk when from a clump of trees on the left side of the road stepped a man with a gun on his hip. Deverell's heart seemed to grab his ribs and shake them like a prisoner shaking cell bars. He pulled his mare to a halt.

"Hello, Squire Deverell," the man said, his fingers

twitching near the butt of his pistol. "Of course, that ain't your real name, is it?"

Deverell let his own hand creep toward the flap of his coat, beneath which his own pistol was hidden. "Who are you, and what do you want with me?" he demanded.

"The name's Raglow. Bill Raglow. You remember that name for as long as you're able, which won't be long. The rest of the world's going to remember it a lot longer. Bill Raglow—the man who gunned down Briggs Garrett."

Deverell said, "Briggs Garrett is dead."

Raglow grinned. "That right? I hear different. What I hear is that Briggs Garrett is you."

Deverell forced out a laugh. "That's loco. Where'd you hear something like that?"

"Didn't really hear it. Read it."

"What are you talking about?"

"Take a look for yourself." Raglow reached behind him and pulled a folded piece of paper from a back pocket. Wadding it with one hand, he tossed it at Deverell, who caught it.

His hands shook as he unfolded it in the waning light. It was the broadside printed by Shapiro. He read the title line and a few lines of the body, then let the paper fall to the ground.

"Brady Kenton?" he asked weakly.

"Never gives no name, but who else could it be?" Raglow said. "Mr. Garrett, I'm right sorry to have to kill you. I'd love to hear you tell about some of them hangings you've done. But you know how it is."

Raglow abruptly drew his pistol and fired. Deverell felt something hot and slicing sear his shoulder as the bullet plowed a shallow furrow. Letting out a piercing yell, Deverell ducked low in the saddle and spurred his horse forward. The mare, spooked by the shot, shied and almost reared. Raglow leveled his pistol again, stepping forward. Once more Deverell spurred, and this time the mare responded. Surging forward, she knocked Raglow to the ground.

Raglow swore and pushed himself up to fire at Deverell as he rode swiftly away. One bullet after another zipped above and around Deverell. Upon hearing shot number six, he jerked his horse to a stop and turned toward Raglow.

Raglow, barely visible in the last traces of daylight, was fumbling for bullets. Deverell spurred the mare, sending it charging forward. Raglow panicked, dropping bullets that just wouldn't go into the chambers.

Deverell barreled down upon him relentlessly. Raglow finally got a fresh bullet in but realized at the same moment that it was too late to fire, too late to dodge. He threw his arms into the air as the mare slammed him to the ground and pounded over him with hooves that felt like hammers.

Deverell rode on over the man, pivoted the mare, and came back again. Raglow tried to crawl away, but the effort was hopeless. Once again the hooves hammered him into the dirt.

A few moments passed during which he lost consciousness. When Deverell ran his mare over him again and yet again, he did not feel it.

Panting, filled with both fear and rage, Deverell finally stopped his repeated trampling of Raglow. He had done it almost unwittingly, out of pure self-protective instinct. Now the sight of the battered body made him feel sick, and he leaned out of the saddle and emptied his stomach.

When that was done, he took several deep breaths and began riding as fast as the mare could run back toward Leadville.

*    *    *

Mary Deverell almost fainted when she saw the blood on her husband's shoulder.

"Oh, Squire, what happened to you?"

"I'm all right, Mary, I'm all right." Deverell turned to Mark Straker. "I believe you now. There's a broadside that's been published—apparently Kenton's work. It identifies me as Briggs Garrett."

"I found a copy of it on the street after you left. I tried to warn you, Uncle," Straker said.

Usually Deverell despised it when Straker called him by that familiar designation, but this time he did not voice his usual protest. "It's not safe for me here now," he said. "One man has already tried to kill me."

Straker's brows lifted. "How did you get away?"

"I ran him down with my horse. But if there's one like him, there's probably a hundred. We've got to get out of this house, right now."

"I know a place we can go," Straker said. "An empty hut, well hidden, out toward California Gulch. The old Darwin place."

"Fine, fine. Let's go, right now. Mary, gather some food, clothing."

Mrs. Deverell took a carpetbag from a wardrobe and retreated quickly to the kitchen to begin packing it with food.

Deverell looked at Straker probingly. "Perhaps I've misjudged you, young man," he said. "I see now you were really trying to give me fair warning. Damn that betraying Brady Kenton—I'll kill him when I see him next! And to think I've kept him under a roof of my own . . ."

"He's already gone from beneath that roof," said Straker. "I ran him out this morning, and challenged him about his accusations about you. He vowed he would make me regret it. Said he would make his accusations in print. I suppose he meant the broadside."

The front door burst open, and a man came in carrying a copy of the broadside in one hand and a pistol in the other. His expression was wild as he lifted the gun.

"It's gone far enough, Straker," George Currell said. "It's time for the lies to end."

# Chapter 29

Straker stepped forward. "What are you doing here, Currell?" His voice was heavy with threat.

"Coming to tell the truth about you, Straker. I can't carry this around in my conscience anymore. These people have a right to know what you're up to."

"You're drunk, Currell," Straker said. Looking back at the Deverells, he said, "He's drunk. Look at him."

"Yeah, I'm drunk. I been drunk for a long time now. It took getting drunk for me to finally get the courage to do what I had to do."

Mary Deverell clasped her hands together. "He's going to kill Squire!" she said despairingly. "Stop him, Mark!"

Straker advanced another step. "Get out of here, Currell. I'm taking my aunt and uncle to safety."

Currell waved the broadside. "Did you write this, Straker?"

Straker said, "Did you hear that? He's not only drunk, he's crazy!"

Deverell, his face white with fear, said, "Currell, say what you've got to say."

"He's crazy! Can't you see that?" Straker said in a near shout.

"I want to hear what he's got to say." Deverell's expression made it clear that his newfound trust in his wife's nephew didn't run very deep.

"Don't listen to him—can't you see he's trying to trick you, Uncle Squire? He's come to kill you because he believes you're Garrett, just like everyone does."

Currell looked at Deverell. "This is Straker's doing," he said. "Straker planned it all. He wants to see you get killed so he can have your inheritance. That means he's got to get Mrs. Deverell killed too."

"No!" Mary Deverell yelled. "That's not true! Mark would never—"

"Hush, Mary," Deverell said. "Let him have his say."

Mark Straker lunged forward, grasping Currell's gun arm and wrenching it up before the drunken man could react. The two closed and grappled, falling to the floor.

The men writhed and struggled for only a moment before the gun went off. The sound of it was very loud in the room.

Brady Kenton tied his tie with a deft twist of fingers and wrists.

Gunnison, already dressed for dinner, combed his hair to perfect neatness in the ornately framed mirror above the bureau. "Seems strange to be dressing to be a dinner guest after what happened today," he said through the door that connected his room to Kenton's. He and Kenton had been at these new quarters in the spacious Chrisman home since earlier in the day.

"It does," agreed Kenton. "But I don't think we're wasting our time by any means. I have a feeling we may find some answers tonight. Mrs. Chrisman seems to have a remarkable interest in making the acquaintance of everyone involved in this situation of ours."

"You think she may know something about Garrett?"

"Perhaps she does. Or perhaps she's just curious. Either way, I hope to know before the evening is over."

After a few more moments, Gunnison asked, "Kenton, who do you think killed Clance Sullivan?"

"I don't know. It could have been anyone with a grudge against him, or any common criminal he might have tried to arrest. Whoever it was, he was clever enough to make use of the Garrett rumors . . . if only he had known how to spell."

Kenton gave a final tug to his tie. "I wonder what Ella Chrisman looks like." So far, he and Gunnison had seen no one but Gableman since their arrival. He had directed them promptly to their rooms without meetings or introductions.

Gunnison, for his part, was wondering more about the young girl he had seen that day in the upper window overlooking Chestnut Street. It had been a distant view, but she had struck him as pretty. He wondered if she would be at dinner, then felt guilty about his thoughts. After all, he was engaged. That put certain obligations upon him . . . even though the engagement had been arranged more by his parents and Glorietta Sweat's than by him and Glorietta. Sometimes he wondered if he shouldn't face the fact he didn't really love Glorietta and call the entire thing off before it was too late.

Gableman met them downstairs. "Please have a seat in the parlor. Mrs. Chrisman will be down to greet you shortly."

They sat down in a side room filled with expensive chairs, carpeted with a thick green rug, lined with heavily varnished paneling. It reminded Gunnison of the parlor of an old New York home, but without the musty smell that tells an old house's age. No building in Leadville was authentically old.

They waited ten minutes. Kenton grew restless, stood, and began studying the paintings on the wall. At last the parlor door opened, and a woman entered. She was middle-aged, striking in appearance, her hair a mix of black and silver. She wore a dress that would have been perfectly at home at the most elegant East Coast soirée.

"Good evening, gentlemen. My name is Ella Chrisman."

"We are honored to meet you, ma'am. I am Brady Kenton, and this is my associate, Alex Gunnison."

After the usual exchange of pleasantries, Mrs. Chrisman said, "Please come this way, gentlemen. Dinner is ready to be served."

And a fine dinner it was, served by Gableman and a very pretty Irish servant girl named Fiona. She came in and out from the adjacent kitchen, green eyes fluttering at Gunnison—or so Gunnison fancied. His heart fluttered in return. This was a house full of beautiful women, and he wondered why the one he had seen in the upstairs window apparently was not to dine with them.

The hostess, who asked her guests to call her Ella, presented herself as an admirer of Kenton's work and asked him many questions about his career. As usual, Gunnison received much less attention, a distant star twinkling unnoticed while Kenton's sun beamed. But it didn't bother him any more than usual, for he was used to being overlooked, and tonight there was the Irish girl to divert him.

Dinner was pheasant and finely spiced vegetables, rich wheat rolls, butter, and a fine pudding. Coffee preceded and followed the wine. When the meal was done, Gunnison and Kenton were content. Kenton had talked through most of the meal, answering questions, describing his most colorful experiences (those, at least, that could be told to a woman of distinction), even talking some of Victoria. It was the first time Gunnison had heard him do so at this length, and there did not seem to be the usual sadness associated with it. Ella seemed to put him at ease. When dinner ended, Gunnison noted that contrary to expectations, the subject of Mickey Scarborough and Briggs Garrett had not come up.

After dinner, Ella showed the journalists the lower level of the house, then took them up to the second floor, much of which consisted of a remarkable library.

"I have collected fine volumes throughout my life," she said. "There are many first editions here, some of great value. And I'm glad to be able to say I've read most. Many collectors are more interested in possessing books than reading them, you know."

"True," Kenton said. "My late cousin Wilfred was such a man. He collected volume upon volume, piling them onto shelves . . . a man purely obsessed. But he seldom read. His books wound up ruining his life. He climbed a shelf one day, looking for Victor Hugo, and the entire stack collapsed on him. Banged up his spine. He was hunchbacked the rest of his days. He finally had to resort to bell ringing to support himself."

Ella looked at Kenton warily, caught the twinkle in his eye, and laughed. "Come," she said. "I have my rarest volumes—including Hugo—locked up downstairs in my office. I would like to show them to you."

Gunnison asked permission to remain in the library so he could further examine the books and perhaps sketch the remarkable room for the *Illustrated American*. The request was gladly granted; it was Gunnison's impression that Kenton and Ella wanted to be alone.

In the library, Gunnison thumbed through books and read countless titles on musty stiff spines. Kenton and Ella did not return. When Gunnison grew tired of the books, he opened the French doors and walked out onto the balcony. It overlooked a yard much larger than he would have guessed. Surrounded by a tall board fence, it extended back a good hundred and fifty feet. At the rear stood a small house—not a shack, but a cottage, tightly built and painted a creamy brown. A light burned in the window.

"Coffee, sir?"

He turned. It was Fiona, standing in the French doors, smiling prettily.

"Yes, thank you." Gunnison took a cup. "How long have you been with Ella—Mrs. Chrisman, Fiona?"

Her pretty brow wrinkled. "Oh, it's been these seven months now," her appealing Irish voice said. "I joined her after Mr. Chrisman . . . departed."

"I see. Do you enjoy your work?"

"Oh, yes. Mrs. Chrisman is a delight. Always kind and fair."

"Tell me—the young woman who lives upstairs, who is she? I saw her at the window recently."

Fiona looked quickly around, as if Gunnison had touched on a delicate matter. She drew closer—which brought no protest from Gunnison. "That is Mrs. Chrisman's daughter, Roxanne."

"Why did she not dine with us?"

Fiona seemed uncomfortable with the question but unable to resist answering. "If I might say so privately, sir, she and her mother have differences. Miss Roxanne keeps often to herself, especially when the Missus is taking on particular hard about poor Jerome, as she has lately."

"Jerome?"

"Yes." She spoke even more secretively. "Mrs. Chrisman's son. That room in there, beyond the oak door is where—"

The library door opened, and Gableman called for

Fiona. She quickly turned on her heel and left Gunnison alone, never finishing what she had started to say.

Sipping the coffee, he leaned against the balcony rail and listened to the sounds around him. Back in the hallway, Gableman was giving some sort of instruction to Fiona; from below, he could hear Kenton and Ella talking, their words indiscernible.

When he had finished the coffee, he took the cup back into the library and set it on a desk. Noting the door to the room Fiona had indicated, he hesitated, went to it, and reached for the latch. It was unlocked. The door creaked open into a small room lined with more books, stacks of newspapers, photographs, old but well-dusted toys. Gunnison picked up a lamp and walked inside.

A rocking chair sat near a coal grate. Above the mantelpiece hung a large photograph of a young man in a Union uniform, a pistol in his hand and laid across his lap and turned up for show. On a little gold plate at the bottom of the frame was the soldier's name: *Jerome Marchbanks.*

Marchbanks . . . but Fiona had said Jerome was Mrs. Chrisman's son. Why was his surname different from hers? Perhaps she had been previously married.

As Gunnison looked around the small room he had the sense of standing in a shrine. There were other photographs, all obviously of Jerome. They showed him at different ages. There were three pencil sketches of a baby that Gunnison assumed was Jerome. The toys must have been Jerome's. The books around the room, when followed from left to right, represented a typical boy's advancement in literary interest, from nursery volumes to folk tales to biographies on up to Dickens. On a separate shelf stood books on military history, the science of warfare, and the speeches of Lincoln.

"Mother sits in here, you know," a voice said.

Gunnison wheeled. A striking girl with long blond hair was standing in the door. "Sits in here, rocks, and broods over Jerome, as if doing that could change anything. It's what finally drove Father away."

She came forward, thrusting out a small beautiful hand. "I am Roxanne Chrisman. You are Mr. Gunnison, I believe?"

"Yes. I'm honored to meet you, Miss Chrisman. I'm sorry you didn't dine with us."

"Mother and I usually dine apart. I dined earlier, in my room."

Gunnison indicated his surroundings with a wave. "I'm also sorry you've caught me where I probably should not be."

"As I said, it doesn't matter. This room is Mother's obsession, not mine. I wish she would close this door forever."

"Jerome was your brother?"

"Half brother. He was born to mother before she married father. That's right—he was illegitimate."

"I see."

Roxanne smiled, a sight worth seeing. "You react more casually than most to that information. Some are far more . . . shocked, maybe? But Mother has never worried about it, so I don't either. Even before Father divorced her, she was accustomed to being perceived as a woman of scandal." She placed an almost mocking emphasis on the last words.

"I take it that Jerome is dead."

"Yes. He was killed during the war. It's been seventeen years, and Mother feels the loss worse now than ever. Time usually heals. In this case it didn't."

"I'm sorry to hear that, Miss Chrisman."

"Please, call me Roxanne."

"Gladly. And you may call me Alex."

Roxanne walked past Gunnison and looked at the

picture of Jerome Marchbanks. "He was handsome, wasn't he? Much like his grandfather."

"His name seems familiar to me for some reason."

She turned away from the picture. "Jerome was his grandfather's namesake. It's the grandfather you've heard of. Doctor Jerome Marchbanks was a Boston surgeon. Very noted. He had a special interest in diseases of the heart. He taught much of what he knew to Mother. With what she knows, she is qualified to be a doctor. But she never took formal training."

"Yes—I have heard of Dr. Marchbanks. I read about some of his work." A thought came to mind. "Roxanne, was Mrs. Chrisman's knowledge of heart trouble the reason she asked for Mickey Scarborough to be brought here after he collapsed?"

Roxanne smiled, but rather sadly. "That's a sufficient enough explanation, I suppose."

Suddenly Gableman strode into the library, looked around, and headed straight for the room the two were in, a very dour look on his face.

# Chapter 30

Gableman fired a harsh glance at Gunnison and then a second, longer round at Roxanne.

"Miss Roxanne, you know this is Mrs. Chrisman's private room. You should not be here, and certainly this young gentleman should not."

"This is my house too," Roxanne said with a trace of defiance.

"Yes, but your mother is the owner and mistress of it, and all of us must abide by her direction, as you know," Gableman returned. He had a voice rich enough to sprout seed. "Come now, both of you."

If Gableman was a servant, he nevertheless carried a tone of authority that made others tend to obey him. Roxanne walked out into the library, and Gunnison followed. Gableman closed the door and locked it with a key hanging from his watch fob. Gunnison set the lamp he had been carrying on the table where it had been.

"Mrs. Chrisman obviously forgot to lock the room herself," he said. "I will hope, Mr. Gunnison, that you will not take all unlocked doors you find as invitations for entry."

"I was in the wrong, and I admit it. I'm trained to be curious, and sometimes I give in to temptation."

"There is no harm done, I'm sure. Now, sir, if you would like a drink, or more coffee..."

What Gunnison really wanted was Roxanne. "Perhaps I can just sit down here and read," he said, indicating a chair beside the lamp table. He hoped Roxanne would remain.

Gableman said, "As you wish. Feel free to select any volume."

Gableman left, and to Gunnison's displeasure, Roxanne followed, giving one backward glance. Gunnison experienced another flash of doubt about his upcoming though still-unscheduled marriage to Glorietta. Was he making a mistake? With girls such as Roxanne in the world, did he want to tie himself down for life just yet?

He got down a copy of *A History of New York,* by "Diedrich Knickerbocker," and tried to convince himself he was reading it when he was just scanning words. Finally he gave up the pretense and put the volume down. He wondered what Kenton and Ella were talking about. Garrett, maybe.

The French doors rattled in a burst of wind, and Gunnison walked over to make sure they were closed. One of them blew open as he approached it, and he noticed again the little house at the end of the long backyard. This time, a woman stood at the door, her form backlit by the interior light. She was emptying a teapot on the ground. She seemed familiar, so Gunnison stepped out onto the balcony for a closer look.

Of course! It was Kate O'Donovan. Obviously the little house was where Ella was putting up the family.

Kate O'Donovan glanced up as he came onto the balcony and studied him for a moment. Gunnison wondered if she had recognized him; probably not, as he was likely too shadowed for her to see.

An exterior staircase on the far end of the balcony led down to the yard, and he descended. Passing a lace-covered window, he noticed Kenton and Ella seated inside in facing chairs, talking intently over glasses of red wine. Neither saw him as he went down the stairs to the yard.

Kate O'Donovan had seen him descend and waited, cautiously, in the doorway, the teapot still in hand.

"Hello, Mrs. O'Donovan."

"Hello, sir," she said. He could tell that she now recognized him. "I was not expecting to see you here."

"Kenton and I are now guests of Mrs. Chrisman, just like you. We lost our other quarters." Gunnison smiled in a friendly way. "It was kind of her to see to your safety, I must say. This seems a hidden enough place."

"Aye, it surely is, though safe I cannot feel anywhere, since the fire."

"You do know that the man who set the fire is dead, don't you?"

"Yes. The marshal told me. For that at least, I'm thankful."

"May I come in?"

She seemed uncertain but nodded after a moment. "Do not be thinking me unfriendly for my hesitation, sir. It's just that Lundy is still such a frightened boy. It's so hard a time now that I think even Old Papa knows something is not right."

"I don't want to disturb Lundy, but I do wish to speak to him. I'd like him to know I still consider him my friend and that I understand why he was slow to tell the truth."

"I suppose you've got the right to see him if anyone does." She stepped aside, and Gunnison entered.

The O'Donovans would surely have preferred to be safe in their former house, but there was no denying their new arrangements were superior. This little cottage was a tightly constructed, well-decorated place, cozy as an oversized dollhouse. Gunnison figured it was Ella's guest cottage.

Lundy appeared at the door leading to the little kitchen on the west end of the rectangular cottage. He looked like someone who had been deprived of a week's sleep. The grandfather was not to be seen, but Gunnison heard a guttural voice from one of the two tiny bedrooms and knew he was there.

"Hello, Lundy."

"Hello." He spoke in a near-whisper.

"It's been quite a rough time for you since we took that walk out to the mine."

"Yes."

"For me too. You heard about the man who tried to kill me—the same man who burnt down your house? He's gone now, you know. Shot to death by a policeman. His name was Johnson. He'll never bother you again."

No words this time, just a nod.

"I want you to know I consider you my friend, Lundy. Mr. Kenton and I are staying in the big house there, for now. If ever you want to come see us, please know you're welcome."

He nodded shyly. Gunnison noted silently how the turmoil of the ordeal had muted the boy's normally exuberant manner.

"I'd best get back to the house now, Lundy. I hope you and your family have a good evening."

This time Lundy grinned, and it was good to see.

Kenton tossed his tie on his bed and rubbed his throat.

"It was a rewarding evening, in two ways," he said, "the first being that Ella is quite a lady, most remarkably attractive." He looked wistful. "A woman like one too seldom meets in the sort of life we lead. Did you know she has as much medical know-how as the average doctor? Her father was a crack surgeon."

"I know," Gunnison said. "I also know Ella Chrisman is at least five years your senior."

"And what is wrong with maturity? Besides, all I said was that she was attractive. I'm not talking about marrying the lady."

"So what was the second rewarding part?"

"Hmm? Oh—simply that I've concluded Ella didn't invite us out of any obsession to find out about Briggs Garrett. It doesn't even seem it was Mickey Scarborough's raving about Garrett that caused her to have him brought to her house. It was just that she realized from the audience that he had suffered a heart seizure and knew she was the most qualified person in Leadville to deal with it. Refreshing, isn't it? You go expecting to find an obsessed woman and wind up meeting one of the most sane persons you've encountered in years."

"To tell you the truth, Kenton, I'm surprised you're not disappointed not to have found more answers about Garrett."

"Well, maybe I am a little disappointed. It's just that it was such a prime evening and a welcome break from all this trouble. . . . What a woman she is! I swear, she's almost as smart as I am!"

Gunnison usually gave scornful replies to Kenton's occasional shows of ego, but this time he let it pass. He knew from having talked to Roxanne that Kenton was wrong on at least one score about Ella Chrisman: She was, contrary to his opinion, an obsessed woman. Her obsession wasn't with Briggs Garrett, maybe, but the idea of her rocking for hours in a room enshrining a long-dead son did not seem all that sane or healthy to Gunnison. He thought about saying something about it to Kenton, but the man seemed so happy that he decided not to. "So she asked you nothing at all about Garrett?"

"Oh, of course she did. We talked about it quite a lot, in fact. It would be almost impossible to hold a conversation in Leadville at the moment without Garrett coming up. But if she was obsessed on the subject, she covered it well."

"If she's as intelligent as you say, then I'd say she could cover pretty well."

"You're a cynic, Alex."

"You've taught me to be. Right now, you seem to have your eyes full of stars." Gunnison wasn't sure why he was, in fact, speaking so cynically. Since his visit to the "shrine" for Ella Chrisman's son, he had felt doubtful about the woman. "Did she ask if you knew who in Leadville is really Garrett?" he asked.

"Yes ... and she asked specifically about Squire Deverell. That shows that the incident with Mark Straker this morning has made it into the local gossip. I was afraid of that—Straker was a fool to say what he did. He probably sparked a lot of speculation about Deverell being Garrett when he yelled his accusation in public. It was almost as if he wanted—" Kenton cut off suddenly, a strange expression on his face. "Merciful heaven, Alex, merciful heaven! Maybe that's it! Maybe Straker was trying to do exactly that!"

"What are you talking about?"

"No time now, Alex. Get dressed again. I'll try to explain it on the way."

"On the way to where?"

"To Squire Deverell's house. We need to have a talk with him, and with Mark Straker. I think I've figured out what's going on here."

# Chapter 31

Someone had tacked one of the broadsides to a post on the street outside Ella Chrisman's house. Kenton was the first to see it, and something about it drew him to it. He read the title line, swore beneath his breath, and yanked the cheaply printed paper from its nail.

"What does it say, Kenton?"

Kenton read for a minute, ignoring the question, then wadded the broadside and tossed it down. "Now there's no question that someone is manipulating this situation. I'll bet my life it's Straker. That blasted broadside is made to look like I wrote it. Straker must be trying to get Deverell killed."

"Why would he do that?"

"Inheritance, if I had to take a guess. And if that's right, that means he'll have to get Mary Deverell out of the way, too."

Kenton explained his suspicions as he and Gunnison continued on a near run toward Deverell's.

Gunnison was awed by the theory, but had to admit it made great sense.

As they progressed, Gunnison began to notice something unusual about the town. The streets were relatively empty, and in the atmosphere was a spark of tension and danger. Gunnison wondered if he was imposing his own feelings on the situation or picking up on something objectively there.

A man approached with a copy of the broadside in hand. "A good service you've done here, Mr. Kenton, if I must say so," he said, waving the paper. "I knew that eventually the truth about Briggs Garrett would come out. 'The truth will out,' that's what I told the Missus. 'The truth will out,' I says."

"It hasn't outed yet," Kenton responded.

The man heard that but didn't seem to grasp it. "There's no name signed to this story, Mr. Kenton—but you're the man who wrote it, right?"

At that, Kenton whirled and faced the fellow, shooting lightning from his eyes. "You are *not* right. Far from it. That paper is the damnedest, most dangerous lie I've had the misfortune ever to see. You spread the word, friend: Brady Kenton had nothing to do with that broadside, whatever you think you've read between the lines. That paper represents an effort to get an innocent man killed."

The man still didn't seem to understand, but there was no time to waste with him. The journalists went on, leaving him blinking after them.

"Blood may flow because of this," Kenton said. "Let's just hope it hasn't already."

Deverell's house was dark when they arrived. Neither was there light in Straker's quarters at the top of the stairs. Kenton knocked on the main door but received no answer.

"This is dangerous," Gunnison muttered. "There's probably people watching the house."

"I know. Come on, let's check the back. Maybe they're hiding out in there. Lord knows Deverell has reason to hide, if he's seen this."

They found the back door locked as well, and the rear of the house as dark as the front.

"Maybe he's gone to safety. We can only hope so," Kenton said.

There was a heavy, crashing sound from inside the house.

"Kenton—"

"I heard it. Stand back. I'm going to break in this door."

It took only one run and heave for Kenton to pop the lock and hammer the door open. The journalists went inside. Kenton struck a match and by its light found a lamp, which he lit. They heard a bumping noise from the front room and carefully edged that way.

Lamplight spilled in and revealed a body on the floor, lying beside an overturned china cabinet. The face was turned away, but both could see it was not Deverell. They went to the prone man and rolled him over. The man, still alive, let out a groan. There was blood beneath him, leaking from a bullet wound.

Kenton held the lamp higher, and light spilled onto the face.

"Currell!"

And so it was. The man's face was pale. A little blood leaked from the corner of his mouth and stained his mustache.

"Who did this to you?" Kenton asked.

Currell's eyes trembled open. "Mark Straker . . . shot me."

"We'll get you help, Currell, right away."

Currell grabbed Kenton by the collar with the unencumbered hand. "No . . . not yet. First you've got to listen to me! Got to hear me out. Straker's got to be stopped."

The man obviously was determined. "Go ahead, then," Kenton said.

"It was Straker behind everything all along... he wants his uncle's inheritance. He's in the will to get it all when Mr. and Mrs. Deverell die. He had that broadside printed so people would think Deverell is Garrett.... You seen it?"

"I've seen it."

Gunnison asked, "Currell, was it you who kept Chop-off Johnson from killing Lundy and me at Deverell's mine?"

"Yes... I wouldn't be part of no more murdering." He stopped, swallowed, moaned from his pain.

"'Murdering'? What are you saying?"

"Listen to me... Straker is bad. A lot of the robberies and such going on, he's been behind them. He keeps a lot of the local footpads supplied with opium, cheap liquor, and such in return for a cut of what they take. A man named Jimmy Rhoder started doing the same at his billiard hall. Straker got mad, went over drunk one night. Lynched Rhoder right in his own building, then set the place afire. Then he paid Chop-off Johnson and me to take Rhoder's body and dump it in Deverell's empty mine. Me and Chop-off thought that when the body was hid, that would be the end of it."

Currell paused, groaning. The exertion of talking was hard on him, but he forced himself on. "When that Scarborough fellow collapsed on stage hollering about Briggs Garrett, the whole town got to talking about it. That started Straker to thinking, trying to figure some way to use those rumors to his advantage. He finally figured a way to cover up Rhoder's murder once and for all and get his hands on his inheritance besides.

"He told Chop-off and me to get Rhoder's body back, put it somewhere where it would be found. That's why Chop-off and me was at the mine that night, Gunnison. Straker's idea was that folks would believe

Briggs Garrett had killed Rhoder, and we would all be free and clear. Then he could spread the rumor that Deverell is Garrett, and somebody would shoot him or string him up.

"Chop-off and me went along with it all, but after it went bad at the mine, Chop-off went loco and decided on his own to get rid of the O'Donovan boy. All that time I was getting jumpy. I wanted out. It bothered me bad that the Deverells would have to die for Straker to get what he wanted. I never cared much for Deverell himself, but Mrs. Deverell, she's a good woman. She don't deserve to be murdered. When I saw that printed paper tonight, I came down here to tell Deverell the truth. But Straker was here—shot me down before I could talk. I think he thought he killed me, but I was conscious enough to still hear him. He took the Deverells off somewhere, telling them he was going to keep them safe. I heard mention of the old Darwin cabin in California Gulch."

Currell was speaking more slowly and softly as he went on, weakening, and there was more blood on the corner of his lip, gurgling up from inside him.

"You've got to stop talking now," Kenton said "We have to get you to a doctor."

"Too late for me . . . just listen to me, please. I passed out after they left. When I came to, I tried to get up on that cabinet and just pulled it over. Thank God you heard it, Kenton. Thank God. Now maybe you can stop Straker."

Wearied by the exertion of talking, Currell relaxed and seemed to sink back deeper into the floor. His eyes closed.

"Don't go out on me, Currell. Tell me how to reach the Darwin cabin."

"Like I said . . . California Gulch . . ." He was fading out fast.

Kenton said, "Currell, I'm sending Alex to find help for you. I'll stay beside you until it arrives."

"No! No time . . . you got to stop Straker . . . before it's too late."

Kenton propped a pillow from the sofa behind Currell's head and covered him with a decorative quilt he pulled down from the wall. "We'll stop him, Currell. I promise you."

Currell spoke without opening his eyes. "You get Straker for me, Kenton. And save Mrs. Deverell. Tell her I was sorry for what I did."

"We'll get you patched up. You'll live, Currell. You'll have the chance to tell her yourself."

Currell did not answer him. He opened his eyes wide, took a deep breath, and exhaled slowly. When the breath was gone, so was the luster of his eyes.

Kenton pulled the quilt up over Currell's face.

# Chapter 32

They found the police station empty.

"They're gone, every last one of them," said the old man behind the desk.

"What's happening?" Kenton asked.

"Ain't you heard? Vigilantes! Going to get Briggs Garrett. They know now who he is, you know—that Squire Deverell fellow. It was writ up on a paper and spread all over town. And we hear that Deverell's nephew what lives with him showed up in town a little while ago and told folks that he couldn't stand to hide the truth no longer. Said Deverell really is Garrett, just like the story said. Now he's going to lead some vigilantes down to where Deverell is holed up. Marshal Kelly got wind of it and has every man out trying like the devil to find where the vigilantes are gathering up."

Kenton and Gunnison left the office in a rush. "We've got to find Deverell before the vigilantes do," Kenton said. "At least we know roughly where he is."

"California Gulch . . . that's Perk Starlin's area, isn't it?"

"Yes, and Perk will know where that Darwin cabin is. Come on—we're going to the stable and get him and some transportation."

*     *     *

The pair found Perk Starlin easily enough and even more easily persuaded him to throw aside his watchman duties at the stable and go with them. Perk was ready at any moment for whatever excitement he could find.

"I know the Darwin place. We'll take the wagon," Perk said. "She's ready to hitch in the back."

"I didn't know you had a wagon," Kenton said.

"I don't. It belongs to Horace Tabor. It's just parked here for the night for safekeeping." Seeing Kenton's expression, Perk seemed offended. "Don't look that way—we ain't going to hurt it none!"

Kenton didn't argue under these circumstances, and within minutes they set off. While the wagon rattled down a dark road, Kenton explained the complex situation to Perk as best he could. Perk, simple as he seemed, was actually keen-minded, and well before they neared the area of the Darwin shack, he had a grasp of what was going on. "Sounds to me like you might ought to let me do the first talking," said Perk. "Deverell won't trust you right now. He does trust me—I guarded one of his mines a few months back."

Perk lifted a finger like a railroad spike and pointed to the east. "The Darwin cabin is right beyond that little ridge. The road curves around. We'll ride in close, and then I'll holler."

"Is that a good idea?" Gunnison ventured.

"Better than surprising him," Perk said. "I'll wager he's got that old pistol of his gripped tighter than a fat lady's bloomers. I tried to buy that pistol off him once, I did. He told me where to go."

By the time they stopped the wagon, Gunnison was shaking and feeling cold, but it was more from tension than temperature. He kept looking back toward the road, waiting for the inevitable procession of men—masked, they would probably be—who would eventual-

ly come down in silent as phantoms, carrying guns and
a noose. He hoped Perk could convince Deverell they
were here to help rather than hurt and get them all out
in time.

They left the wagon and went to the top of the
ridge. The cabin stood below. It was dark, but they
could feel presences there in the blackness below.

"Do what you can, Mr. Starlin," Kenton said.

Perk cupped a hand to the side of his mouth and
yelled: "Mr. Deverell! You in there?"

Silence. Then the rattling of a shutter, the click of a
pistol hammer. Gunnison noticed how loud things like
that can sound to someone tense and scared in the
darkness, smelling danger like a stench in the air.

"Mr. Deverell, it's Perk Starlin! Listen—I come
here to help you. I hear you're in a sort of a bad spot
right now."

More silence. But suddenly Deverell's voice came
riding up on the breeze. "Is that really you, Perk?"

"In the flesh. You got to listen to me, Mr. Deverell.
Mark Straker has got you fooled. He didn't bring you
out here for safety—he brought you out to get you in a
good isolated spot for a lynching. You understand?"

Again there was no sound, but they could all but
hear the clicking of Deverell's mind as he took it all in.

"Think about it, Mr. Deverell—has Mark Straker
ever done anything good for you before? Has he ever
looked out for anybody but himself? He wants you
killed, and your Missus too, so he can get your
inheritance."

A pause. "How can I know who to believe?" Deverell
called back. "You might be out to get me! I can't trust
anyone!"

"Mr. Deverell, you were always square with me
whenever I dealt with you, and I'm being square with
you."

"How'd you know where to find me?" Deverell yelled, still sounding suspicious.

Perk looked over at Kenton, not knowing how he could respond to that without mentioning Kenton. Kenton, for once, seemed at a loss for an answer. But before the pause became long enough to seem suspicious, Perk called back, "It was Straker! He's telling folks in town where you are. He's going to bring a bunch of vigilantes back here! Didn't you wonder why he cut out and left you here so quick?"

"He said he was going to get us more food," Deverell said. "It did strike me kind of strange."

The wind was soft but sounded loud there in the noiseless night. All at once, a new voice spoke—Mrs. Deverell, sounding loud and upset. She was talking, pleading with her husband. Those outside could make out only what fragments the shifting wind happened to carry their way. The gist of it was clear, though: She didn't trust Perk Starlin, and Deverell did.

Finally Deverell said over the protesting voice of his wife, "We're coming out!"

Kenton reached over and patted Perk on the shoulder, grinning. Perk looked pleased with himself.

Light from a newly lit lamp rose in the windows, then the cabin door swung open and the Deverells stepped out. As Perk had predicted, Deverell had a big pistol in one hand. In the other was the lamp. Mrs. Deverell was clinging to him and looked wilted and feeble there on the dark porch.

Perk stood so they could see him, and waved. Right then Gunnison heard something on the road behind, a sound from far away carried on the wind, making him think of wartime and military advances by night.

It was the noise of tramping hooves.

\*       \*       \*

When Deverell saw Kenton, he gave the look of a man betrayed and raised his pistol. "I knew I shouldn't trust you," he said to Perk. "That man there may well be the very reason I'm in the fix I am."

"I had nothing to do with those rumors or that broadside," Kenton said. "Mark Straker was responsible for both."

Deverell lowered the pistol a little. "Currell said the same thing."

"Listen!" Gunnison said.

The sound of approaching riders was a little louder than before, though still distant.

"Hear that, Deverell? That's a lynch mob," Kenton said. "I guarantee you that at the head of it is Mark Straker, putting on a show of pretended sorrow that his uncle is really Briggs Garrett. I'm sure he's told the crowd about how sorry he is to have to turn on his own blood kin but that for the sake of justice, he'll make that sacrifice. Straker is a snake, a liar, a Judas. Come on, Deverell—let's get you out of here while we can!"

"There's heaps of old empty feed sacks and stuff in the back of the wagon. We can hide the Deverells under there," Perk said.

"And Alex and me too," Kenton said. "I think our presence out here at this time of night would be difficult to explain to those vigilantes, thanks to that damned broadside."

Mary Deverell appeared to have given up. She leaned on her husband, who had by now let his pistol arm sag back toward the ground again. He looked as drained and weak as his wife.

"What if they want to search the wagon?" Gunnison asked.

Kenton bit his lip, thinking. "I wish I had a good bottle of whiskey right now."

Perk said, "I got a flask in my pocket, though it

seems a right bad moment to be taking time out for a drink."

"In this case it's not for drinking, just for spilling," Kenton said.

Perk, a confused look on his face, reached into his pocket and came out with a half-full flask of cheap whiskey that he handed to Kenton. Kenton opened it, walked over to Gunnison, and began pouring liquor down the inside of his shirt. Gunnison yelped in surprise.

"Take a good mouthful and swish it around so your breath will smell of it," Kenton said. "What worked one time might work a second—if we can dirty your face enough to keep Straker from recognizing you." He wet his hand with whiskey, reached to the ground, brought up a handful of moistened dirt, and smeared it on Gunnison's face.

The younger man began to understand what Kenton's idea was and gave himself a good mussing. In the meantime Kenton quickly explained his plan. When he was done, they went to the wagon. Kenton and Gunnison helped the Deverells into the back and covered them with empty sacks, then they too crawled under.

"I can hear 'em clear now," Perk said from the driver's seat. "You all stay good and still, hear?"

The wagon lurched out onto the road again. When they were a hundred yards from the old shack, Perk began to sing loudly "Bringing in the Sheaves." For a coarse old watchman, he had a surprisingly decent voice.

# Chapter 33

Beneath the cover it was difficult to breathe, and what air the hidden ones sucked into their lungs was filled with dust and grit from the feed sacks. Gunnison fought to stifle insistent urges to cough and sneeze.

They rolled along, buried in cloth and darkness, hearing the creak of the wagon wheels on the road. Above it all was Perk's voice: ". . . by and by the harvest, and the labor ended, we shall come rejoicing, bringing in the sheaves!"

Now Gunnison heard something else and sensed the presence of others. The silent vigilantes were approaching; he knew it even though he couldn't see them. The others knew too; Gunnison felt Mrs. Deverell tense beside him, felt her husband patting her hand.

Perk began a new selection, one that did nothing to put anyone at ease: "In the sweet—by an' by—we shall meet on that beautiful shore . . ."

The wagon creaked to a stop. Perk stopped singing. Everything was far too silent for a quarter of a minute. The vigilantes and Perk were facing off.

"Good evening, gentlemen," Perk finally said. He lifted his now nearly empty whiskey bottle. "Care to scour your gullet a little?"

"No." The voice, filtered through a mask, was humorless and sandy. "Who are you?"

"I'm Perk Starlin. Best watchman west of Denver. Dang good wagon driver, too."

"And a drunk, it would appear." The speaker sounded disgusted. Whoever this vigilante was, Gunnison found him peculiarly moralistic for a man heading out to take the life of another without trial or real evidence.

"It so happensh I am a drunk, sir," Perk slurred back. "My father wuzza drunk, an' my grandmother afore him."

Nobody laughed. "What are you doing out here this time of night?"

Perk turned up the flask, drank the last swallow, then belched loudly. "I wash wondering the same about you fellowsh, masked up an' all like you are."

"You answer my question." One of them shifted in a saddle and levered a rifle.

"Well, to tell you truth, I jush been out drinkin'. Ain't nothin' to brag on, I know, but ish the straight fact."

"You came all the way out here just to drink?"

"Well, yeah. Man gets drunk in town, he c'n get arreshted."

"What's in the back of the wagon?"

Every muscle in Gunnison's neck became hard as granite; he felt as stiff as a cemetery statue.

"Jush some feed sacksh."

"Well, you won't mind us taking a look, then."

Gunnison's moment had come. Sending up a silent prayer, he let out a loud sputtering cough, groaned, and sat up, pushing aside the feed sacks that had covered his face and chest. "Perk, whash happenin'? Whur are we?" He hoped his drunken slur was as convincing as Perk's had been.

"We met us shome frien's on the road, Willie,"

Perk said. "These gents're out getting some fresh air and wearin' corn-meal sacks over their headsh ta keep their ears warm." He gave an inebriated cackle.

"Who is this?" the vigilante leader demanded.

"That there's my frien' Willie Smith. Him and me wash drinkin' tagether." Perk took on a worried look. "He ain't like me—comes from good family. He's gotta repatation. Gets back to his daddy that he was out drinking, an' ish hell to pay for him. That's why I didn't tell you about him. You won't tell, will you?"

The leader peered at Gunnison through holes in sackcloth. He shook his head. "Have you been near the old Darwin cabin?" he asked Perk.

"We rode close by, we did."

"Any sign of life about it?"

"Seems we shaw a light, didn' we, Willie? Thash right—we sure did see a light there."

The vigilante leader waved his hand. "You two get on. Forget you saw us, and we'll forget about you. Not a word, understand?"

"I didn't see a thing, mishter. Not a shingle thing. You, Willie?"

"Notta thing." Gunnison coughed again and tried to look as if he might get unpleasantly sick at any moment.

"Get on, then," the man in the mask said.

The vigilantes filed past on both sides. One stopped and looked at Gunnison for a couple of moments. Like the others, he was masked, but Gunnison knew beyond question it was Mark Straker, looking at him, thinking he looked familiar. Gunnison rubbed his hand over his face as if he were scratching it. Straker looked a moment longer, then went on. He had a coil of rope over his shoulder. Ironic, but not surprising, that he should be the one to carry it.

The last of the vigilantes went past. Perk drew up

the lines and prepared to start off again. At that moment, Mary Deverell gave a loud, feminine moan from beneath the piled feed sacks.

"What was that?" one of the vigilantes asked. The entire group had heard it. They wheeled, came back toward the wagon.

The leader came to the side of the wagon and looked at Perk. "That was a woman's voice, and don't deny it. Who else you got under there with you?"

He reached into the wagon.

"No!" Gunnison bellowed, totally at a loss about what to do. Mary Deverell moaned again.

"Pull back those sacks!" the man ordered.

"I can't . . . she's . . ."

Perk cut in. "She's a little short of clothes if you gotta know. Willie's a little too respectable to flat out shay something like that, but thash what it comes down to. She kind of, huh, well, somehow lost 'er skirts today."

Gunnison could almost read the disgust on the man's face right through his mask. "Drunks and harlots. We ought to hang you all right here. Pull back those sacks like I said."

"You might not oughtta do that," Perk said. "This gal ain't no harlot."

"What are you talking about?"

"Just that she comes from one of yer good Leadville families. Her daddy, he'd be right embarrashed if this here situation got out in public. We pull them sacks back, and one of you very gentlemen is liable to look here in this wagon and see his own little girl, drunk as a shailor and missin' her skirts." He paused and looked over the now-silent group.

"Pull those sacks back!" came a voice from farther back. It was Mark Straker's.

Perk shook his head resignedly. "If you gentlemen are sure . . ." He reached into the back of the wagon.

"Leave it be," the leader snapped quickly. "Get out of our sight, get back into town and try to find forgiveness for your evil ways."

Perk put on a bright face. "Now I shee! You gents are in some sorta church! Them ma-masks, they something you wear when you're doing holy things?" He grinned as if oblivious to the irony of his own words.

"Get out of here—and forget you saw us. Otherwise we'll come looking for you, and we won't be lenient."

"Good evenin', genmun."

The wagon lurched away. Perk burst into a chorus of "Onward, Christian Soldiers." Gunnison lay back, gasping in relief, saying a prayer of gratitude that Perk was so quick a thinker and convincing a liar.

When the wagon had gone a sufficient distance, Kenton rose. "I hope you realize how close we came to a noose right then," he said. "Perk, let's get a move on. When they find that cabin empty, they'll come back looking for us."

Mary Deverell moaned again,. Squire Deverell rose and pushed away the sacks. Mary Deverell did not rise; she moaned all the louder.

"What's the matter with her?" Kenton asked crossly. "She almost got us killed back there!"

Deverell was in tears. "It's not her fault," he said. "Mary has a bad heart, and I think this has been too much for it. We've got to get her some help, or I'm afraid I'll lose her!"

Kenton said, "I'm sorry, Mr. Deverell—I didn't know."

Gunnison said, "Kenton, if it's her heart—"

"Ella Chrisman?"

"Yes."

"Good thinking, Alex. Perk, we've got to go to the house of Ella Chrisman, Chestnut Street. If there's any way to approach from behind, or by some less obvious way..."

"I can manage that," Perk said. "You folks hang on—we're going to speed up now, and it may get bumpy."

He snapped the lines and sped down the road.

# Chapter 34

Ella Chrisman's well-featured face was golden in the lamplight as she leaned back in her chair. She wiped a strand of gray hair from her forehead and stood. Before her on a high-backed bed lay the frail form of Mary Deverell.

"She's going to be fine, I believe," she said. "Her heart doesn't appear to be the problem. An emotional collapse is a more likely explanation."

"She had grounds for one," Kenton said. He nodded at Deverell, who stood on the other side of the bed. "Well, sir, things appear brighter. I'm glad for it."

"I must speak to you, Kenton," Ella said.

"Of course."

Gunnison had also been in the room and now left with them. Ella gave him a look that said he was not invited to listen to what she had to say. "I think I'll take another look in the library, if it's all right," he said, then excused himself.

Ten minutes later, Kenton also came into the library. Gunnison put down the book he had been flipping through.

"Ella is concerned about the danger of keeping the Deverells here. I can hardly blame her," Kenton said.

"So what will she do?"

Kenton smiled. "As I've said before, she's quite a lady. She's decided to let the Deverells stay anyway. No one knows they're here except those of us here, and Perk. They should be safe enough for now. In the meantime, we need to find Marshal Kelly, tell him what happened with Currell, and show him the body."

"You think the vigilantes are still out looking for Deverell?"

"By now they're probably returning to town. Straker is likely pretty mystified about where his intended victims went."

Gunnison smiled at the thought. "I'd say it won't take them long to think back to that wagon with the two drunks and the hidden 'girl.' I'll bet they—"

Gunnison stopped talking, for a look of horror had just come over Kenton's face. "My God, Alex," Kenton said, "we've been fools! We should never have let Perk leave here!"

Perk had in fact left shortly after sneaking his wagonload of passengers to the Chrisman house. At the time none of them had thought better of it, distracted as they were by the condition of Mrs. Deverell. But now Gunnison realized, as Kenton already had, that Perk could be in significant danger, for he had identified himself by name to the vigilantes. Probably at least some of them already had known him anyway and that he served as night watchman at the James Stable.

"What can we do, Kenton?"

"Go find him, of course. Marshal Kelly will have to wait until we know Perk is safe."

They stayed in the darkest places and avoided the open street as they headed toward the stable where Perk worked. When a fire wagon came clanging by, they ducked into the inky blackness of a recessed doorway. When the wagon had passed, they stepped out again and looked in the direction it had gone.

"Look!" Gunnison pointed toward the sky.

The clouds were lighted by flames. A house was burning, and from the amount of fireglow, it appeared to be a big one.

"Deverell's house, blast it!" Kenton said. "I'd say Straker set it himself after he got back into town. He'll blame it on nameless vigilantes, of course."

"But in the meantime he'll have destroyed Currell's body," Gunnison said. "Still covering his tracks."

When they reached the stable, all was dark. "Maybe Perk realized they would come looking for him and went elsewhere," Gunnison said.

"We can only hope. But let's look inside to be certain. Look—the gate is unlocked. I don't like that. I don't believe Perk would have left it that way."

It was so dark inside the stable that Kenton and Gunnison almost stumbled across each other twice. When they were in far enough that a light would not be readily noticeable from outside, Kenton struck a match.

Immediately Gunnison recoiled and let out a yell.

Perk was hanging in front of him, not a yard away. At first he thought Perk had been lynched but then saw he actually was hanging by one arm. His feet were bound, and below his bootsoles the rope was looped in a slipknot. Just to the side lay a feed sack that obviously had just been removed from the loop. Perk's eyes were closed, and he hung limp, unconscious or dead.

Kenton said, "Let's get him down from there."

From around the corner came Mark Straker, a pistol in his hand. With him were two other men, both with the look of men accustomed to the cut of life's roughest edge. One of them held a pistol; the other had a knife sheathed in his belt. Gunnison figured them for two of the footpads Straker had on his hook. One of them lit a lantern and held it up.

"Don't worry about your friend, Kenton," Straker said. "He's unconscious, that's all. Hanging by one arm with a sack of feed tied to your ankles generates quite a lot of pain, I assure you. But he didn't snap, this one. He wouldn't say where he took Deverell. Denied ever having him, though I don't believe that for a moment. That feminine moan—I have no excuse for not recognizing it as Aunt Mary's. A clever liar, this watchman is." Straker looked at Gunnison. "Hello, 'Willie Smith.' I thought that young drunk in the wagon looked familiar." His eyes shifted over to Kenton. "Were you in that wagon too?"

"Yes I was. Under the sacks."

"You're a brave pair, that I grant. Let's hope you're as talkative as you are courageous. Tell me what you've done with Uncle Squire."

"We took him back to his house. If that's his place burning out there, likely he's burnt up with it," Kenton said.

Straker smiled and shook his head. "A nice bluff, but it doesn't wash. When we came back from the Darwin shack, the group went to look for Uncle Squire. I went back to the house and set it afire."

"To cover your killing George Currell?" Gunnison said.

Straker's face darkened, and Gunnison knew he had made a mistake. Now Straker would have even more reason to get rid of him and Kenton.

"No more bluffs; no more games," Straker said. "Tell me where you've taken Squire Deverell!"

"You won't get that out of us any more than you got it out of Perk here," Kenton said. "I'll not betray a man to be murdered just because you threaten me."

Straker's eyes narrowed; he was obviously studying

Kenton. "You know, I don't believe you would, Mr. Kenton." He holstered his pistol and reached to his boot. From it he drew a long knife. "Let me tell you what my offer is, Mr. Kenton. You tell me where you've stashed Uncle Squire, and I'll use this knife to cut down Perk Starlin. You don't tell me where he is, and I'll cut Perk open like a slaughtered beef, gut to gullet. I'll spill his innards right on this floor. Now—what's your choice?"

Kenton had always been a fast reflexive fighter, and though Gunnison had often heard him complain that middle age was lessening his speed, he surely gave no evidence of it with his next move. His foot shot up and kicked Straker's knife hand; the move reminded Gunnison of an oriental fighting style Gunnison had once seen demonstrated at an exhibition in New York. Straker didn't let go of the knife, but he would have been smarter if he had. His hand flew up and back, and he actually stuck the blade into his own right shoulder. He let out a scream.

His assisting footpads, fortunately, were not fleet fellows. Gunnison whirled and grabbed the pistol held by the closer one. The footpad lost his grip on it, but Gunnison had jerked it so quickly, he couldn't keep his either. The pistol flew from his grasp and straight into the lantern held by the second footpad. The lantern shattered and spilled burning fuel down the man's legs.

The man screeched pitifully, flung the shattered lantern into an empty stall, and took off on a run for the door. His flaming legs were crisscrossing streaks of glowing orange. He cut around the edge of the door, still screeching. Making for the closest water trough, Gunnison figured.

Kenton, meanwhile, had his arms wrapped around Straker, who had dropped his knife and was trying to reach his pistol. Kenton was keeping him from it, but looked as if he were losing his advantage. Straker was younger and not nearly as fatigued as Kenton.

"I'll help you!" Gunnison yelled, and darted forward. But the other footpad grabbed his collar and pulled him back. His head thudded against a post.

Next thing Gunnison knew, he was rolling over and sitting up, rubbing his head. His vision was cloudy water slowly going clear. When the clouds were gone, there was Kenton, backed up against a wall, pinned by the footpad while Straker thrust his pistol under Kenton's chin.

"Where is Squire Deverell?" he demanded.

"Go to blazes," Kenton spat back. Straker thumbed back the hammer.

"Wait," Gunnison said, struggling to his feet. "Wait. I'll tell you."

"Don't do it, Alex," Kenton said. "Don't tell him!"

Gunnison stood, faltering, wanting to save Kenton but also loath to betray the location of the Deverells. In only a moment, however, the decision was taken out of his hands, for from the doorway came a feminine shout: "No!"

Gunnison wheeled. It was Roxanne Chrisman.

"Roxanne! Get away from here!"

"No, Alex! I'll not see you or Mr. Kenton killed." She faced Straker. "If you want to know where Squire Deverell is, I'll tell you. He and his wife are both at my mother's house. The house of Ella Chrisman."

# Chapter 35

Straker smiled.

"You're most cooperative, young lady. You can cooperate even more by stepping further inside—else you'll see this man die." He gestured at Kenton.

"Don't do it—run!" Kenton directed.

She did not seem to know whom to obey. She hesitated, then came inside. Meanwhile, flame was spreading all around the stall into which the footpad had thrown the shattered lantern. Choking smoke billowed.

Straker grabbed Roxanne when she drew close. "You're hurting me!" she protested, struggling in his arms.

Kenton, meanwhile, was still pinned by Straker's remaining crony. Gunnison, though unrestrained, could do nothing as long as Straker threatened Kenton. Perk Starlin still hung by his dislocated arm in the center of the stable. Now he groaned, beginning to stir back toward painful consciousness.

"I seem to have the advantage here," Straker said.

"I don't think so," Kenton replied. "What are you going to do with us? Kill us all? You can't afford that

kind of risk, and you know it. The stable is burning—
one man has already run out of here with his legs afire.
You think we're not going to draw attention within
moments?"

Straker was angered. "Shut up!"

"Not until I tell you something you need to know.
George Currell lived long enough to give a full report
on the murder of Jimmy Rhoder and all your subsequent doings." At first, Gunnison was surprised Kenton
had revealed that information to Straker, but his next
words made clear the bluff he was pulling. "He talked
to Marshal Kelly before he died—he knows everything
now. They'll be looking for you. You've worked yourself
into a corner you can't get out of. Give it up."

"I said shut up!" Straker yelled. "I'll kill you here
and now!"

"No you won't. It would only make it worse for
you."

"I will kill you—the girl too!" Straker returned. He
was obviously losing control of his temper and common
sense.

The footpad holding Kenton suddenly let him go.
"You ain't paying me enough to step into something this
deep," he said to Straker. "I'm getting out."

Straker's eyes were wild. Without a word, he lifted
his pistol and shot the footpad through the head. The
man fell in a dead heap. Roxanne struggled harder.

"Brilliant—a gunshot!" Kenton said. "Now I know
we'll get lots of attention. And look—the flames are
climbing the wall. Fire fighters and police will be here
at any moment. You're through, Straker. Give up and
they'll go easier on you."

Straker swore and waved his pistol about. "Burn!
All of you burn! I'm taking this one and getting out
while I can!"

He dragged Roxanne on her heels to the outside,

then swung the door closed. The fire had spread into two more empty stalls and now was crawling along the underside of the roof. Horses kicked and struggled as the heat grew more unbearable.

Kenton bolted for the door Straker had just closed and found it jammed tightly shut from the outside. Suddenly Perk Starlin fell to the dirt floor, the rope trailing after him. The end of it had been tied to a wall post in one of the stalls that had caught fire, and the flames had eaten through the hemp.

The jolt of the fall knocked Perk awake and popped his dislocated shoulder back into place at the same time. He let out a fearsome yell, grabbed the shoulder, then rose to his knees, looking around in incomprehension.

"Alex, come help me with this door!" Kenton yelled. The smoke was growing thick. Horses stamped and screamed louder than before, pounding themselves against the sides and doors of their stalls.

Gunnison joined Kenton, and together they pounded the jammed door. It began to yield. Whatever Straker had jammed it with cracked and broke. The door swung open.

On the other side of it stood Straker, his expression that of a man who had just looked his own death in the eye. He stumbled forward toward Kenton. "Help me," he said. "Help me."

Into his back was deeply thrust a broken-handled three-tine pitchfork. The handle bobbed up and down each time he moved. He collapsed facedown, the broken end of the handle pointing straight up.

"Kenton . . ." The voice was Perk's and sounded weak.

Kenton and Gunnison ran back and helped Perk to his feet. Through the black smoke they made it out of the stable. Then Kenton turned and disappeared into the hot murk again.

Perk collapsed outside. "Save the horses," he said. "Get somebody. . . pull down the back wall and save the horses!"

But Gunnison did not respond. He was waiting for Kenton to emerge with Straker from the smoke-filled doorway. Suddenly a terrible crash came from inside the building, and an explosion of flame. The ceiling was beginning to fall in.

"Kenton! Oh, Lord, no . . ."

Others were there now. Perk, still worrying over the horses, led several men around to the back of the burning structure where they began pulling away wall boards to get at the stalls from behind. Gunnison remained oblivious to it all, even to the touch of a feminine hand to his as Roxanne walked up to his side.

"I'm so sorry," she said softly.

Only then was Gunnison aware of her. "Roxanne . . ."

A figure emerged from the smoke, coughing, staggering, but still on his feet. "Kenton!" Gunnison yelled joyously. "You're alive!"

He went forward. His big partner put a hand on Gunnison's shoulder to steady himself. "Couldn't save . . . Straker," he gasped. "He was pinned under the roof timbers."

"You tried, Kenton. That's a lot more than Straker would have done for you or anyone else."

Kenton turned and watched the flames eat away the big wooden building. The firemen had arrived now, coming straight from the fire at Deverell's. As the firemen went to work, Kenton noticed Roxanne.

"I don't believe I've had the pleasure," he said.

Gunnison said, "Kenton, meet Roxanne Chrisman. Roxanne, meet Brady Kenton."

Roxanne extended a slender hand. Kenton's muscled dirty paw closed over it. "Was it you who put the pitchfork into Straker?" he asked.

"Yes. He pushed me down and told me to stay there while he jammed the door shut. He said he would shoot me if I moved. I moved anyway. The pitchfork was leaned against that tree—I just grabbed it and ran at him."

"You're a brave young woman. Your mother should be very proud of you."

Roxanne's eyes widened. "Mother! Oh, no, Mr. Kenton—in all that's happened I've forgotten why I came after you in the first place. Hurry—we've got to get back to the house before it's too late!"

"What's happening?"

"I think Mother is going to kill Squire Deverell. Oh, please do hurry!"

"Kill Deverell . . . why?"

"After you and Alex left the house, Gableman brought Mother a broadside he found posted on the street. It says that Deverell is Garrett, and Mother believes you wrote it. She said you must have written it and that you must have lied to her when you told her Deverell wasn't really Garrett."

"We know about the broadside," Gunnison said. "But why does Ella care?"

"Because of Jerome! Jerome was one of the bridge burners Briggs Garrett hanged and burned!"

"Jerome . . . Jerome Marchbanks?" Kenton asked.

"Yes!"

"I remember the poor boy. . . I had no idea he was Ella's son."

"Come back to the house, quickly!" Roxanne urged again. "It may be too late already!"

As they ran up to the Chrisman house, the door opened as if by magic. A very frightened Fiona appeared.

"Hurry—she and Gableman have got him in the backyard, and if you don't stop her, it's going to be terrible!"

"Where is Mrs. Deverell?" Kenton asked.

"Asleep in her room—please hurry! The Missus has a rope and coal oil, and she's going to do to Deverell what she says he did to her son!"

They bolted through the house and into the backyard. There they stopped, staring at a most unusual scene.

Deverell stood on a barrel, a noose around his neck. The rope was tied to a branch of the lone tree in the yard. Deverell's hands were bound behind him. Gableman, looking very uncertain, stood nearby, a torch in one hand and a pistol in the other. At his feet was a capped coal oil jug.

Beyond, Lundy and Kate O'Donovan stood in the doorway of the guest cottage, watching the scene in horror. Lundy was clinging to his mother, his face half buried in the folds of her nightgown.

Ella Chrisman, who had been standing and staring silently at the pitiful Deverell, wheeled when the group entered the yard. She lifted her arm and pointed at them. "Stay away!" she demanded. "Stay away unless you've come to witness the settling of accounts after seventeen years!"

"Mother, you can't do it!" Roxanne said. "It would be murder!"

"No worse a murder than the one that stole my son from me! A murder of the murderer himself—that's justice. The vengeance of the sufferers!"

Kenton stepped forward. "Squire Deverell is not Briggs Garrett," he said.

Ella Chrisman shook her head violently. "So you say in your spoken words, but I've read your written ones. Why you withheld the truth from me I don't know, but now I have the one I've wanted so many years!"

"I didn't write that broadside. It was written by the nephew of Mary Deverell so that Deverell would be wrongly identified as Garrett and killed. Then, after some covert murder of Mrs. Deverell, Squire Deverell's inheritance would pass to the nephew. It was a clever, evil scheme, but it's over now."

"I don't believe you."

"I can prove that Deverell is not Garrett. Garrett should have a scar across his chest, the mark of a saber slash I gave him the very day your son died. Open his shirt, Gableman. I think you'll find not a scar upon him."

Gableman looked at Ella. She glared at Kenton but nodded curtly.

The tall black man stepped forward. The entire group drew near. It was almost dawn; the eastern sky was growing milky and light.

Gableman reached up and ripped open Deverell's shirt. The light of the torch revealed a long scar running diagonally down the exposed chest.

Kenton was so stunned, he stumbled back two steps. "Garrett!" he said in a whisper.

Deverell's jaw trembled. Tears brimmed in his eyes. "I'm not Garrett," he said. "That scar has been on my chest since childhood. I fell from a barn loft and cut myself on a nail—it's no saber slash."

His words had no vigor. He spoke them obviously believing they would make no difference.

Kenton was speechless. Finding the scar on Deverell's chest was the biggest surprise yet handed him in a week overflowing with surprises.

"Now you see!" Ella declared joyfully. "He *is* Garrett!"

Kenton stepped forward again, looking into Deverell's

face. "No," he said. "Scar or no scar, I can't believe this man is Briggs Garrett."

But Ella Chrisman had stopped listening. She walked forward and looked with a perversely delighted hatred at Deverell. "You will die as my son died, Briggs Garrett. I thank the heavens for delivering you into my hands. Gableman, bring the coal oil."

"No! In the name of the Virgin, no!" It was Kate O'Donovan. She was running across from the cottage, sobbing and crying out. "You must not, Mrs. Chrisman. You cannot do this to an innocent man!"

Ella, completely taken aback by this development, stared at Kate O'Donovan for several moments. "This is not an innocent man—he's plagued your life as well as mine. You should want to see him die, Mrs. O'Donovan."

Kate was frantic. "No!" she screamed. "No!" She stopped, collected herself, and wiped her tear-stained face. "I feared this day would come," she said. "Sometimes I let myself hope it would not . . . but now I can hope that no longer." Then to Ella: "If it's Briggs Garrett you must have, then have him you shall, and if the hate in you is so great that you can bear to hurt him more than God already has, then into your hands I give him. May God forgive me if what I do is wrong."

She turned and walked slowly back into the cottage. Lundy fell back against the wall and sank until he was sitting on his heels. He buried his face in his hands as she passed him.

The watching group was confused. Only Kenton seemed to have a glimmering comprehension of what was happening. He had gone pale in the rising morning light.

Kate O'Donovan rolled out the old man in the wheelchair, bumping across the lawn until he sat directly before Ella Chrisman. "Here he is. Do with him what you will, if you have it in you to punish a man heaven has already stricken."

Kenton walked forward. All were silent as he stooped and opened the old man's shirt and revealed the long ugly scar that ran like a frozen lightning bolt down his chest, much more pronounced than the scar on the chest of Deverell.

Kenton looked at the scar, then lifted the old man's chin and peered intently into his face. After several moments he closed his eyes and turned away, nodding.

The sun was above the horizon now, spilling down the light of a new day.

# Epilogue

*One month later—Austin Bluffs*

Victor Starlin lit his pipe carefully in the shadows of his cabin. When the tobacco was glowing ruby red, he gave a thoughtful grunt. Across from him, Brady Kenton sat in a chair tilted against the wall, having just finished telling Victor the full story of the "Leadville incident," as he had begun calling the adventure he and Alex Gunnison had shared on the other side of the Mosquito Range.

"So Scarborough really did see Briggs Garrett in his audience," Victor said. "Imagine what that must have been like, looking out and seeing a face that familiar, and that despised, on the body of a mindless old man in a wheelchair. No wonder Scarborough was jolted. And all that followed . . ."

"All that followed resulted from a combination of coincidence, manipulation, and the public's eagerness to believe shocking things," Brady Kenton said. "That, and the nosiness of a little Irish boy who didn't even know his 'Old Papa' was really a legendary outlaw and the obsession of a willful woman who had spent seventeen years brooding over the death of her illegitimate son."

"But how did Garrett get into the condition he is, and how did the O'Donovans wind up with him?" Victor asked.

"It all had to do with Lundy's late father, who must have been a fine and merciful man," Kenton replied. "According to Kate O'Donovan, Jock O'Donovan was at the same flooded river crossing where Garrett reportedly was drowned. All that happened no one seems to know, now that Jock O'Donovan is dead, but the end result was that O'Donovan crawled out of that flooded river barely alive and dragged with him a fellow victim who was in even worse condition. The man had struck his head on something when the flood wall hit and badly bashed his skull. Young Mr. O'Donovan took such pity on him that he took him into his own care, all the while trying to determine his identity. When he found out the fellow was none other than Briggs Garrett, he and his wife faced a difficult choice. They could turn him over to the law, or they could keep him under a new identity. They had come to love the fellow, so they chose the latter—and so Briggs Garrett became 'Old Papa,' a man everyone, myself included, naturally assumed was the father of either Mr. or Mrs. O'Donovan. Lundy was just a young sprout when all this first happened, so he never knew who 'Old Papa' really was."

"Didn't it disturb the O'Donovans that the man they had taken in was guilty of the kind of crimes Briggs Garrett did?"

"I asked Kate O'Donovan that very question. Her answer may not make a lot of sense to you, but to me it does, because I've seen what Briggs Garrett is now. She says she doesn't see him as the same man he used to be. The Briggs Garrett who was evil and cruel, she said, is dead and gone. He was, for all practical purposes, drowned at that river crossing, just like all the newspapers said. What was left behind was Briggs Garrett as he once had been in the only days of innocence he ever knew."

"In other words, his infancy."

"Exactly. Briggs Garrett, when it comes down to it, is no longer a man but a child. And a child he'll be for the rest of his days, being cared for by a woman and boy who love him dearly. Strange, isn't it, how things happen sometimes."

Victor Starlin reached over and picked up the latest copy of *Gunnison's Illustrated American*. On the cover was one of Kenton's finest drawings. It showed a smoking railroad bridge and seven dangling bodies. In the foreground was a picture of a man with a saber. His face was unseen, shadowed by the brim of his hat. Above the scene were the words: *THE SEARCH FOR BRIGGS GARRETT: A TALE OF PUBLIC DECEPTION IN LEADVILLE, COLORADO.*

"You could have drawn the face in, Kenton," Victor said. "You now know very well what Briggs Garrett looks like."

"Yes, I suppose I could have. And I could have told the real story in print, just like I've told it to you. As a journalist, telling the real story is what I am naturally inclined to do. But sometimes there are things more important than stories. Things like giving people a chance to forget, and to heal."

"Ella Chrisman, for example?"

"Yes. She's in Denver now, on an indefinite visit with some relations. The Garrett incident struck her hard. She found that when she faced Briggs Garrett in the condition he was in, she could no longer muster enough hate to harm him. So she just let him go. Now it's going to be up to her to try to let seventeen years of brooding go as well. It won't be easy for her, but she'll succeed. She's a strong woman." Kenton smiled mischievously at his old friend. "And not bad to look at, either, Victor. She's the first woman to really catch my eye since I first saw Victoria all those years ago."

"If Ella Chrisman is reflected in her daughter, I daresay she's quite a beauty," Victor Starlin replied. He rose and went to a nearby window and looked out at Alex Gunnison and Roxanne Chrisman, who walked together on the surrounding grassy level, hand in hand. "Looks like you may lose your partner to marriage, Kenton. Did the kin of his previous fiancée take it hard when he broke off the engagement?"

"The Sweat clan? Oh, yes indeed. They wailed to high heaven. It was hard enough for them to find someone willing to obligate himself to poor Glorietta the first time around. Now they've got to start looking all over again. I'm sorry for them, but I'm mighty glad for Alex. Roxanne is quite a catch."

"That she is. Thanks for bringing her out to meet me."

"We tried to get Perk to come out as well, but he wouldn't do it. Squire Deverell has given him a job as an ore-wagon driver, and Perk's taken to it just fine."

"I'm amazed. Perk's never had a real job in his life. Never seemed to want one."

Victor went to the wood stove and knocked out his pipe. "It's strange to think of Briggs Garrett, still alive and living in the midst of a town that will never know who he really is."

"It is strange, I admit. But I couldn't reveal him, Victor. I just couldn't."

"I understand, and I don't fault you for it. But how did you finally convince the people of Leadville that Squire Deverell wasn't Garrett?"

"Through the help of Ella Chrisman and a man named Allen from one of the local papers. Ella kept the

Deverells hidden until Allen and I were able to get
hold of Deverell's old war records. He fought for the
Union and was at the Shiloh fight, among others. He
had quite a good record as a soldier. Allen published it
all, and Deverell was finally able to come out of hiding.
He received lots of apologies, let me tell you, but he
didn't take them very well. He's still a snappy old
terrapin. But he's taking good care of Perk and giving
Mrs. O'Donovan a lot of work as well. There's a good
heart beating inside all that sourness."

"There's one thing I'm still not sure about, Kenton,"
Victor said as he refilled his pipe. "Who killed Sullivan,
the policeman?"

"A good question, and one of the mysteries that
will probably remain unanswered. My guess is that
Chop-off Johnson did it. Clance Sullivan was probably
following him or worrying him in some way. Marshal
Kelly himself found an old shack up behind the mines
where Sullivan was strung up. It appeared that Chop-
off had been holing up there."

"Speaking of Kelly, what's his attitude toward you
now?"

"His attitude is that he hopes Brady Kenton stays
far from Leadville for a long time. And I intend to make
him happy, because I don't have any ambition to return." He paused. "At least not until Ella Chrisman
does . . . and then all Kelly's men won't be able to keep
me away."

From outside came the sound of a chorus of bleats
mixed with the music of singing Mexican voices as
Victor Starlin's shepherd drove their sheep back in for
the night.

Starlin grinned. "Let's have some supper," he said.

If you enjoyed THE HANGING AT LEADVILLE
by CAMERON JUDD, be sure to look for
his next novel for Bantam,

# CHEROKEE JOE

Here is an exciting preview of this new western
novel, to be published in January 1992.
It will be available wherever Bantam titles
are sold.

Turn the page for a sample of CHEROKEE JOE
by Cameron Judd.

The hog charged and rammed its victim for the ninth time just as another .44 slug ripped through the shed wall. Joe Wolfkiller, a swarthy young man with long, black hair and broad, high cheekbones sculpted by the Cherokee half of his ancestry, grimaced and thrust his face down into the mucky straw in which he lay. Splinters and grit from the punctured wall rained down upon and around him. The hog retreated, squealed, charged a tenth time, then withdrew to the rear of the bullet-riddled shed, grunting and slobbering.

Slowly Joe Wolfkiller lifted his head. His face was dabbled with mud and manure and whiskered with straw. He lay behind a heavy foundation beam about ten inches high, the only piece of wood in the shed thick enough to protect him from the bullets being sporadically spat toward him from the tiny house across the clearing. Cautiously he peered through a knothole toward that house.

Smoke drifted around a north-facing window. He saw movement behind the broken glass and thought of rolling closer to the shed door so that he could return fire out of it. But the impulse was fleeting. Joe Wolfkiller, for once in his life, didn't want to fight, just to get away. His antagonist, a usually harmless, potbellied no-account named Hambone Coltrane, was not a man he wished to harm. In fact, Joe was used to thinking of Coltrane as a friend, or at least one of the closest facsimiles of one he had known in a largely friendless experience. Only when Coltrane was drunk and dejected, as now, did he turn sour and threatening . . . though never before had he gone so far as to try to gun down his companion.

Behind Joe, the hog grunted loudly and sank down into the reeking, moist straw. Joe glanced back; tiny bloodshot eyes glared back at him, full of fear and an animalistic approximation of hate.

Coltrane's voice came from the house. "You dead yet, Joe? You dead yet?"

Joe Wolfkiller put his mouth close to the knothole and shouted back: "Not dead—but this hog will be if you keep shooting!"

No answer. Silence hung heavy. Some instinct warned Joe, and he buried his face in the filth again, digging deep into the foulness as another shot blasted the knothole into a ragged gash and passed through the shed to knick the hog's left ear.

The beast rose, squealing in pain, and charged Joe again. This time it bit him on the calf, lifting his leg and jerking its head from side to side like a wolf trying to rip meat from a fresh kill. Joe let out a yell as he tugged free.

"Got ya that time, Joe, got ya!" Coltrane shouted triumphantly, misinterpreting the meaning of Joe's yell.

Joe Wolfkiller had no time to answer, for the hog was on him again, ramming and grunting and voicing porcine sounds of threat. Joe could take no more. He rolled onto his back, aimed his mud-grimed Colt, and squeezed the trigger.

The bullet took instant effect. The hog's pink eyes widened and dulled. It fell heavily to the side, a little rivulet of blood flowing from the bullet hole between and slightly above its eyes.

Joe rolled to the left and lay staring at the animal. Maybe he shouldn't have killed it, he thought. Now Hambone Coltrane really would be furious. He had always loved that hog.

"Joe?" Coltrane sounded uncertain. He had heard Joe's shot. "What'd you do just then, Joe?"

Joe wiped his pistol on his denim trousers. "I killed your hog, Hambone," he yelled through the wall.

A pause. "What did you say, Joe?"

"I said I killed your hog."

In a moment a great muffled wail of grief reached Joe's ears. He dug himself down into the strawy mud floor again, knowing what would follow.

This time Coltrane fired three shots in quick succession, puncturing a wallboard with the first two and knocking it clean out with the third. Still vibrating, it fell back atop the dead hog. As the noise of the gunfire echoed away Joe heard Coltrane cursing in a voice hoarse with weeping.

Joe rolled back to the right, then heaved up and over the dead hog, using its warm mass for cover. Peering up over its side, he eyed Coltrane's tiny house through the gap where the wall plank had been. He looked for Coltrane behind his window and did not see him.

A moment later the house's single door opened and Coltrane came dashing out, carrying his smoking rifle, his ample belly jiggling as he ran toward the roughly built stable diagonally across the clearing. Coltrane wore galluses but no shirt. His greasy trousers rode so low that the upper part of his buttocks pooched up above the baggy seat.

Joe recognized his best opportunity to shoot his foe but did not take it. He still had no desire to harm Hambone Coltrane—and he actually felt guilty about having had to kill Coltrane's beloved hog. It was a novel feeling, for Joe Wolfkiller seldom felt guilty about anything.

I'm sorry about the hog," Joe yelled at the running man. "It was trying to eat my leg off."

By now Coltrane had reached the stable. Joe wondered if Coltrane planned to go around the stable and approach the hog shed from the side or rear. That theory was shattered by a shot from inside the stable. A terrible, trumpeting whinny followed, then a dead thud. With a burst of horror Joe realized what Coltrane had just done.

"You shot my horse, Hambone!" Joe yelled.

"It was fair—you kilt my hog!" Coltrane yelled back. "You had no call to kill my hog!"

Joe became fiercely angry, raised his pistol, and impulsively fired a shot through the stable. Immediately he wished he hadn't.

"Hambone! You all right?"

Hambone Coltrane, obviously unscathed, emerged from the stable and pounded heavily back to the house. Joe lowered himself again behind the dead hog, wondering how long this foolish standoff would continue.

For a long time there was no sound except the wind and wails from the house as Hambone Coltrane grieved over his hog. Joe thought about Coltrane's slaughter of his horse and became more philosophical than furious about it. The horse hadn't been hard to come by, after all—he had stolen it, and its saddle, too, a month before. His biggest regret was that now the horse was dead he had no good means of escape. There was always Hambone's mount, of course, but that was nothing but a balky mule whose fastest clip was a weary lope.

Joe thought about kicking out a rear wall plank, squeezing through to freedom, and making a run on foot, but he feared Hambone Coltrane would come after him, which could only result in him having to shoot Hambone, or vice versa.

So he just lay there, hiding behind the dead hog. Minutes passed; the day waned and the March air began to cool, the hog cooling right along with it. Joe watched shadows outside stretch east toward Missouri, growing longer and darker as the sun traveled westward and down. A gopher skittered across the clearing. Joe began to feel tired.

Hambone Coltrane's curses and moans became softer and less frequent. Joe watched the window carefully, looking for sign of Coltrane repositioning himself to shoot again. Every now and then he would see Coltrane's face look out, but no shooting ever followed. Finally, as dusk came, Joe concluded that Coltrane had finally gotten over his anger, or maybe drunken himself into a stupor.

Standing inside the shed, keeping his eye on the house all the time, Joe stretched his stiff legs and moved his body from side to side. All the filth that covered him now had dried to a thick crust, stiffening his pants and long dark coat and scabbing his skin. He longed for a good wash.

Softly Joe walked to the door of the shed. Still watching the house, he stepped out and into the dusty clearing. Noiseless and light as cattail fluff in the wind, he crossed to the stable.

His horse was dead, like Coltrane had said. Joe looked at it regretfully. At least he still had the saddle, which lay on its side in the corner of the stable. He picked up the saddle and heaved it onto his shoulder.

Joe was sure now that Coltrane was asleep or passed out, so he grew less cautious. Thus he was surprised when the door opened and Hambone Coltrane came staggering out. Joe dropped the saddle and drew his pistol.

Coltrane came right on toward him, carrying something. Joe saw it was his saddlebags, which he had taken into the house prior to the card game that had led to this altercation in the first place.

"I seen you leaving, Joe," Coltrane slurred, sounding meek as a puppy now. "I knew you'd want these here bags." Coltrane's face, from what Joe could see in the early-evening darkness, was puffy and red. His eyes were swollen from drinking and crying about the hog. Coltrane glanced down at the pistol in Joe's hand. "You don't need that, Joe. I don't want no more trouble with you."

"You wanted plenty of it before," Joe said, keeping the pistol right where it was.

"I know and I'm mighty sorry," Coltrane said. He had put on a shirt sometime before and swiped the crusty sleeve of the left arm under his rheumy nose. "I didn't never want to hurt you, not really."

"Drop the saddlebags and move over yonder," Joe said. "And keep where I can see you."

"Joe, don't treat me so—you got nothing to worry over from me."

"You gave me plenty to worry over in that hog shed. And you've killed my horse."

Coltrane sniffed again. "I was wrong to do it. I admit it." A tear rolled down his face.

Joe was repulsed. He disliked drunks and trusted them less, and Coltrane was proving to be one of that particularly unstable kind who swing from mean to maudlin. Joe figured he could just as easily swing back to mean again.

The last thought made Joe realize how unwise it would be to set out on foot, leaving Coltrane with a mount. The man might turn on him again and try to chase him down in the dark. "I'm taking your mule," Joe announced.

Coltrane nodded as if he had expected nothing else. "It's fair payment for what I done, I reckon."

"Payment, but not fair payment. The horse you shot was worth a lot more than that mule," Joe replied sourly. He felt wronged by the disparity of value; it was his way to take bitter note of wrongs done him while overlooking those wrongs he himself did to others. At the moment he had all but forgotten that the slain horse was never honestly his own to begin with.

"I'm a sorry old soul, Joe. I've always knowed I was." He blubbered, almost ready to cry again. "You was right to shoot my hog, just to punish me for the way I done you."

"I shot it to keep it from taking a bite out of me, that's all," Joe replied. "You can get some meat off it, at least." He holstered his pistol and went to the stable. He led out the mule and began saddling it.

"Can't bring myself to eat that hog," Coltrne said. "My Maudie loved it when it was just a little pink thing. Treated it like a house pup that winter she died. Ever since I laid her away, that hog's always put me in mind of Maudie." He choked as a sob welled up.

Joe Wolfkiller had no time to listen to a grown man crying over either a dead hog or a dead wife. He finished his saddling and mounted. The mule, not used to so light a rider, moved its ears and seemed bewildered.

After some goading, the mule finally began to step forward. Joe kept Coltrane in the corner of his eye, just in case he had a pistol hidden on him and had done all this to get an opportunity to shoot on the sneak. He didn't. His fleshy figure looked rather pitiful there in the darkening clearing.

"Good-bye, Cherokee Joe," Coltrane said as Joe began to go out of sight in the dark.

Joe Wolfkiller made no reply. The mule plodded along through the thickening Kansas night, the wind growing more chilly.

It was by the name Cherokee Joe that the twenty-two-year-old half-breed named Joe Wolfkiller was best known in the Indian Territory and up into Kansas. He had never been particularly fond of the nickname, but he was proud of the growing infamy attached to it.

Joe had known from childhood that a life of trouble lay before him. He had been able to smell it coming like a good hunter could smell a deer or buffalo. His father, a full-blood Cherokee named Sam Wolfkiller who raised Joe alone after his white mother died giving him birth, had also foreseen his son's destiny and worried over it. Sometimes young Joe had been able to see his father's concerns reflected like the firelight in the deep black of his eyes. Such visions had never disturbed Joe. If strife and trouble were to be his lot, let it be. He would not run from it. He would drink deeply of it, slake his greatest thirsts on it, thrive from it.

Such an attitude, predictably, had made Joe's anticipations and Sam Wolfkiller's worries self-fulfilling. Before he was into his teens, Joe Wolfkiller was known as a fighter and troublemaker among his young peers in the Cherokee Nation of the Indian Territory. Before he was twenty, he was suspected in a string of thefts and beatings. One of the latter had nearly proven fatal to the victim. To the chagrin of the law and many of the Cherokees themselves, there was never enough evidence to prove Joe's guilt, even though no one doubted it.

The authorities had thereafter kept a close eye on the half-breed who the soldiers at Fort Gibson began calling "Cherokee Joe." The fact that he was neither fully Indian nor fully white was enough to make many distrust him; that he was prone to violence and criminality made him unlikable as well. The older he grew, the more Cherokee Joe had found himself at odds with the world around him.

Joe had been on the run for many months now, living by his wits on the grasslands of Kansas, making or taking a living however he could. It had been a new accusation of crime that drove him away from his home near Tahlequah. The charge was attempted murder; the victim was a troublesome roughneck who had tangled with Cherokee Joe several times. Now the roughneck would do nothing for the rest of his days but sit silently in a chair, staring and drooling.

At this time, ironically, Joe was innocent. The man who had administered the beating was the outlaw Caul Slidell, with whose gang Joe had ridden on occasion. Slidell, who like many of his ilk frequently hid out along the rivers and ravines of the Indian Territory, had never liked Cherokee Joe enough to let him fully affiliate with his select band of "hellriders," as he called them. Joe suspected that Slidell had deliberately set him up to appear guilty of the beating.

The mule plodded through the darkness. Joe's belly was empty and grumbling, but he had no food. He swore at himself for not having thought to take food from Coltrane.

At last a distant sparkle of light off to the west caught Joe's eye. He knew the source of the light. It was the lantern hanging out front of Shadrah Camp's Boardinghouse and Restaurant, which, along with a handful of houses, stood beside a livery stable and mercantile store where two dirt roads crossed here in the southwestern portion of Sedgwick County.

Joe was tempted to make for the light. It meant food, a bath, shelter, maybe a game of cards. Countering the temptation was the fact that he had little money and could easily run into the law or some other source of trouble at a public stop like Camp's.

He halted the mule, weighing his options, and temptation overruled prudence. He justified the decision to himself with the thought that maybe, at the little community, he could find a way to replace Coltrane's mule, by trade or theft, with a more worthy mount.

He called the mule a foul name and goaded it forward. The flicker of light grew brighter and closer, and when Joe was near enough to catch a whiff of beef stew wafting out of the café, he was as trapped as a sailor whose ears had caught the song of the Sirens.

Joe hitched the mule, then paused at the window of the café and examined its occupants before going on to the door. He recognized no one.

The door was homemade of rough lumber but beautified somewhat by a pane of red-and-white-checkered glass. Joe paused to gather his long hair in his hand and tuck it up under his wide-brimmed hat. In his youth, the teachers at the Indian Agency school had made him cut his hair short. Now he wore it long in defiance of them and their world . . . but when a man's belly is empty, Joe had learned, sometimes it was best to put defiance aside long enough to find a meal.

The door creaked as it opened, and everyone inside turned to watch Joe enter. From the lifting of brows and the subtle movements of the corners of mouths, Joe knew he was rousing interest.

Proprietor Shadrah Camp, a beefy man in armbands and an apron, wiped his fingers on a towel and stepped up to him, lowering heavy brows that constituted the only hair on him from the neck up.

Camp's flyspeck eyes looked Joe up and down. "You can't come in here all filthied up like that, boy," he said. "Take you a wash at that trough yonder, if you want in here."

Joe held Camp's gaze a few seconds, then turned so abruptly that Camp was startled into a backstep. Joe heard the patrons inside give a titter of laughter at Camp's undignified reaction.

Ignoring the cool air, Joe stripped off his jacket and shirt at the trough and washed his skin in the dirty water. He washed his hair out, too, and let the wind dry it partially before he tucked it beneath the hat again. By now the muck on his pants and shirt was dry enough to mostly flake off; what remained he was able to remove partially by dabbing the dirtiest spots with trough water.

When he was as clean as he could get, Joe dressed

again and returned to the café. This time Camp did not try to stop his entry, though he did glance down at Joe's hip, clearly wondering if there was a pistol under the long coat. He opted not to ask.

The meal, which would cost Joe almost all his money, was salted ham, potatoes, biscuits, and coffee. Joe was halfway through with it when the glass-paned door opened again. When he saw the man who walked through it, he sat down his coffee cup and reached for his pistol.

The newcomer was named Tom Pease, and Joe knew him well.

# ELMER KELTON

☐ 27713-8 **THE MAN WHO RODE MIDNIGHT** $3.99

☐ 25658-0 **AFTER THE BUGLES** $2.95

☐ 27620-4 **HANGING JUDGE** $2.95

☐ 27467-8 **WAGONTONGUE** $2.95

☐ 26147-9 **THE BIG BRAND** $3.50

☐ 25716-1 **CAPTAIN'S RANGERS** $3.50

---

Bantam Books, Dept. BOW2, 414 East Golf Road, Des Plaines, IL 60016

Please send me the items I have checked above. I am enclosing $_____ (please add $2.50 to cover postage and handling). Send check or money order, no cash or C.O.D.s please.

Mr/Ms _____

Address _____

City/State _____ Zip _____

BOW2 –9/91

Please allow four to six weeks for delivery
Prices and availability subject to change without notice.